Rosemary's Gravy

A We Sisters Three Mystery

USA TODAY Bestselling Author
Melissa F. Miller

Brown Street Books

This book is a work of fiction. Names, characters, places, and incidents either are the product of the author's imagination or are used fictitiously.
Any resemblance to actual persons, living or dead, is entirely coincidental.

Copyright © 2015 Melissa F. Miller

Published by Brown Street Books.

Brown Street Books ISBN: 978-1-940759-10-4

ACKNOWLEDGMENTS

As always, I'm grateful to my editing team—in particular, Louis Maconi. Several good friends read early drafts of this book and held my hand through the 'Oh no, why did I decide to start a new series?' moments. Heartfelt thanks go to my husband and kids for once again fending for themselves around deadlines. Thanks to Andy Brown for his fantastic cover design.

For my Dave

One

THE DAY I WAS FRAMED for the murder of a movie star started out like an ordinary day.

I was up to my elbows in pomegranate seeds when Felix, my client's impossibly hot stepson, strolled into the kitchen and flashed me a toothpaste-commercial-white grin. As usual, he was coming straight from swimming his morning laps in the infinity pool, which sat right at the edge of the canyons separating the Hollywood Hills from the commoners below. Also as usual, he hadn't bothered to towel off, let alone get dressed. So he was basically naked and dripping water all over the terrazzo floor.

"Morning, Rosemary."

I pinned my eyes on his to avoid letting my gaze travel down his tanned, muscled body. It wasn't easy. "You're wet, Felix. Careful you don't slip on your way out."

I consider myself to be a generally friendly person, particularly for a scientist, but something in Felix Patrick's frequent, mostly-naked appearances in my place of work turned me into a flustered mess. I resisted the urge to push my glasses up on the bridge of my nose. Considering I haven't worn glasses since I traded my coke-bottles for contacts in high school, it wasn't too hard to ignore the old urge. But the impulse took me right back to a time when I was an awkward geek girl. Felix had that effect on me.

"Trying to get rid of me already?" He reached his long arms above his head, interlaced his fingers, then engaged his core in a deep stretch that set his muscles rippling and would have made even my youngest sister Thyme, the yoga master, jealous.

I coughed to cover a stupid giggle that was trying to escape my mouth. "No, I'm just busy. You know, working. Do you need something?"

"I'd love a glass of your awesome tangerine juice."

I stifled a groan and wiped my stained hands on my apron. The entire Patrick family was hooked on the citrus juice that I laboriously hand squeezed every morning. Sure, it was deliciously sweet, with depth and just a hint of tangy goodness. But it took a mountain of tangerines and nearly an hour to yield a single pitcher. It had gotten so that my hands started to cramp and ache whenever I saw the color orange.

Stop whining, I ordered myself as I reached into the refrigerator and pulled out the heavy crystal pitcher full of juice. Romantic comedy sensation Amber Patrick and her family could drink a river of the stuff if they wanted to. After all, the demanding movie star was paying me two hundred and fifty dollars an hour to whip up whatever meals her organic, vegan, gluten-free heart desired. She was my ticket out of debt and the holistic private chef business and back into the chemistry lab where I belonged. I should have been spending long hours researching the feasibility of creating metallic hydrogen, not wringing every last drop of juice out of a pile of tangerines.

I poured a scant shot of the liquid gold into a juice glass and handed it across the vast marble island to Felix.

He gulped it down so quickly that I doubt he even tasted it. Then he slammed the glass onto the counter with a satisfied sigh. "Ah, sweet and juicy. Just like someone I know."

There was no way I was going to respond to *that* comment, so I returned my attention to the translucent, ruby-colored gems in the bowl in front of me.

"What's that?" he asked, leaning in to look.

He was so close I could smell the pool chemicals mixing with his coconut-scented sunscreen.

"Pomegranate seeds. They're for the appetizer for your mother's dinner party tonight." Locally harvested organic mushroom caps stuffed with pomegranate seeds and spinach. They were delicious. They'd be even better if Amber would let me add the goat cheese needed for just a hint of creamy richness, but that was a non-starter. Her frequent dinner guests had the dubious pleasure of following her restrictive diet.

"She's not my mother," Felix said stiffly, all his flirtation instantly vanishing. His face clouded.

"Right, sorry. I meant stepmother."

He didn't bother to respond. Instead he bolted from the kitchen without a backward glance, leaving a trail of water for the maid, Alayna, to mop up.

Relieved to have the distraction of Felix out of the kitchen, if not my mind, I turned to roasting the white sesame seeds for the chili garlic sauce that I planned to pair with the adorable baby eggplant I'd picked up at the market the day before. My cell phone chirped. I dumped the seeds into the bowl with the dried chilies and checked the display: *Sage*.

Yes, my middle sister's name is Sage. My aging hippie parents went for the trifecta and named their three daughters Rosemary, Sage, and Thyme in homage to Simon and Garfunkel's "Scarborough Fair."

"Hey, Sage," I said as I checked the time. Nearly eight-thirty, so it was almost eleven-thirty in South Carolina. Her charges were probably sitting down to lunch.

Sage was working as a nanny – excuse me, attachment parenting consultant – for a well-heeled Hilton Head Island society family. Muffy Moore, wife of PGA golfer Chip Moore, was a true believer in the attachment parenting philosophy. The problem was that all that baby wearing, co-sleeping, and playing with Waldorf-approved cloth dolls really ate into her Junior League meetings and charity circuit galas in neighboring Charleston. Enter Sage. For a cool one hundred dollars an hour (plus room and board in the guest house), she did everything short of breast-feeding the Moore brood while their mama kept up her appearances and made the society page every week.

"Can you talk?" she asked.

"Literally just for a minute. Amber's having a dinner party tonight."

"Oh, too bad. Guess you can't sneak out for your Five Guys burgers, huh?"

"Shut up!" I hissed, as if someone might hear her end of the conversation and discover my dark, fast food, meat-eating secret.

As a chemist turned holistic chef, I can make a compelling argument for eating a locally sourced, plant-based diet. Having been raised on a strict regime of tempeh, homemade yogurt, and very crunchy granola, I can also make a compelling argument for all things in moderation, including the occasional bacon cheeseburger with jalapeños and mushrooms. And by "occasional," I mean daily.

Sage ignored my freak-out. "Tell me about the soirée. Is Hottie McSonny Boy going to be there?"

The scene in the kitchen flashed through my mind. "His name is Felix. I'm not sure he and Amber have the closest stepmother-stepson relationship."

"Weird. Given how close they are in age, you'd think they'd be besties."

I tried to hold back a snort of laughter. Felix was twenty-two, the same age as our baby sister, and Amber was twenty-five. Just a few months younger than me. His dad, of course, was in his fifties; I'd say the age difference was stark, but, you know, Hollywood.

"She's having the cast from *Kiss Me, You Fool* over to celebrate. The movie wrapped last week." *Wrapped?* Hearing myself spout Hollywood lingo so casually made me want to gag.

Sage gasped sharply. "You mean you're making that gross vegan food for *Clay Carlson?*"

I ignored the suggestion that my cooking might not be good enough for America's heartthrob *du jour*. Even if being a chef wasn't my calling, my food was good – really good, despite all the limitations posed by Amber's dietary restrictions.

"Actors don't eat anyway. They nibble. In extreme cases, they just inhale deeply." As I shared this sad nugget of information, I reminded myself to contact the inner-city homeless shelters to find one willing to take the obscene quantities of uneaten food that would no doubt be left when the party ended.

"Still. How lucky are you to get to hang out with all those celebrities?"

If she only knew. I envied her, spending her days laughing and giggling with two adorable little kids. Whatever else you could say about the Moores, they seem to be a fairly well-adjusted and loving family considering how filthy rich they were. And unlike *some parents* they didn't force-feed their children a diet of fruit-based cookie substitutes and daily meditation rituals. Yeah, it's possible I'm still bitter about my childhood.

"Anyway, I only have a second. What's up?" I asked, pushing aside the navel-gazing thoughts.

"How'd you like a visit from your favorite sister?" Her voice rose with excitement.

"Thyme's coming to Los Angeles? When?" I needled her. The truth is that all three of us are pretty tight – probably a result of our being so close in age and having been homeschooled with no other available playmates.

"Har har. Seriously. Chip is playing in the Hollywood Celebrity Pro-Am this weekend. He's already out there playing practice rounds. Muffy decided this morning she wants to fly out to watch the event and hit Rodeo

Drive for some shopping. Skyler and Dylan asked to come, too, so we're all coming."

"That's awesome." I felt a smile spreading across my face.

"I know, right? I miss you."

I missed her, too. I missed both of my sisters. We used to get together every other weekend, rotating among our apartments in Boston, DC, and New York. But last spring, our parents' luxury eco-resort ran into financial trouble. Their response? They "gifted" the three of us the business and sailed off on their catamaran into international waters out of the reach of their creditors. Now my sisters and I were scrambling to pay the bills and facing a five-hundred-thousand-dollar balloon payment that would come due at the end of the year. It was enough to make a girl wish for diamonds in the soles of her footwear.

Thyme had been able to find a gig in Manhattan, but Sage and I had both had to say goodbye to our cute single girl pads and pull up stakes. The logical move would have been to walk away, but despite all the weirdness of our childhood, something about the seaside compound had a pull over all three of us. Out of some strange mixture of obligation and nostalgia, we'd agreed to save the resort. I'm sure Thyme, our resident psychologist, could tell me what that said about us. I made a mental note to be sure to never ask her.

Now instead of biweekly girls' nights, we met once a quarter for a funereal conference with our grim-faced accountant and a quick tour of the resort to make sure the managers we hired weren't stealing *too* much from the nearly empty coffers. It wasn't nearly as much fun as trying new cocktail recipes and watching 90s movie marathons, let me assure you. But it was what we'd committed to do.

"Hey, do you want to meet Amber while you're out here?"

She squealed. "Do you mean it? Yes!"

"Consider it done," I promised. Of course, as it turned out, Sage would never get to meet her Hollywood idol. By the next morning, Amber would be dead. And I'd be the prime suspect in her murder.

Two

I WAS SLICING AN EGGPLANT into perfect rounds when Felix reappeared. He was fully clothed, which somehow managed to be a simultaneous relief and disappointment.

"Hey, I want to apologize for losing my temper earlier," he said, giving me an easy smile.

"Feel free." I kept my eyes on the cutting board and maintained my slicing rhythm.

"Feel free to what?"

I paused mid-cut and stared right into his emerald green eyes. "To apologize. You said you want to apologize, so go ahead."

He laughed uncertainly. "I thought I just did."

I felt my eyebrows shoot up my forehead and my mouth twist itself into a knot. My sisters call that my 'cut the crap' face. "Felix. Come on."

He threw up his hands in mock surrender. "Okay, okay. I'm sorry. I'm really, truly, *deeply* sorry that I snapped at you, Rosemary."

I tried to suppress my smile, but my mouth had its own ideas. "Apology accepted."

"Good. I just hate it when people call that whore my mother."

Did he just call Amber a whore?

"Um..."

He must have realized that I was completely flustered by his character assassination of my boss because he quickly said, "Listen, let's just change the subject."

"Let's," I agreed.

He flashed me another bazillion-watt grin. Then he leaned over the counter and pointed at the bowl of salted water sitting to my left. "Are you soaking the eggplant?" He furrowed his tanned brow in apparent confusion.

I wanted to tell him to stop that before it wrinkled his skin. Instead I said, "Yes. If you add salt to the water, it draws out some of the bitterness." I dumped a handful of rounds into the cold water.

"Interesting." He nodded somberly, like a first-year chemistry student at a lecture.

I half-expected him to whip out a notebook and jot down the cooking tip. Maybe he was a closet foodie. "Do you like to cook?"

"Me? Have you ever seen me cook?"

I thought for a moment. "I believe you popped some popcorn. Once."

He leaned toward me, laughter in his eyes, and whispered, "Only because you told me to make my own damn snack."

I flushed. It's possible I may have said something like that early on in my employment, before I'd grown accustomed to a gorgeous, rich boy hanging around my kitchen.

"That's not ringing any bells," I lied before hurrying to change the subject. "Anyway, you seem really interested in food."

His eyes darkened with intensity and he lowered his voice an octave, almost to a growl. "I'm not interested in food. I'm interested in *you.*"

I almost dropped my knife. My heart started to gallop around my chest like a gerbil going full tilt on one of those exercise wheels. I stared at him and tried to breathe. He leaned closer, so close I could feel the soft cashmere of his v-neck sweater brushing against my bare arm, and then ...

Roland "Pat" Patrick strode into the room like he owned the place, which was probably appropriate seeing how he did, in fact, own the place.

Felix jumped back from the counter like it was on fire. "Dad, hi."

Pat glanced at his son and frowned. "For Chrissake, Felix, why aren't you at the studio doing something productive instead of loafing around here bothering the help?"

The help? I swallowed hard and smoothed my face into a neutral mask, but my grip on the eight-inch knife in my hand tightened.

Felix's eyes flashed.

On the one hand, it gave me a warm, fuzzy feeling to know that Felix was prepared to defend me. On the other, more realistic, hand, I couldn't afford to lose this job because of some misguided chivalry or whatever Felix had in mind. I had to defuse the situation, and fast.

I turned toward Pat, gave him a big, cheesy grin, and used my most solicitous tone of voice. "Do you need something, Mr. Patrick? A snack? Or maybe a cocktail? I could make you a gin rickey the way you like them."

For the record, the way he liked them was straight Hendrick's gin poured into a glass. No ice. No fresh lime juice. No club soda. But I guess for the sake of appearance we couldn't just call it a 'big old tumbler of gin.'

He declined the offer with a curt headshake. "Amber said to change the menu for tonight."

"She did?"

"No. I just thought it would be a good use of my time to make a pretend menu modification because I don't have anything better to do."

Out of the corner of my eye I saw Felix balling his hands into fists.

"I'm sorry," I said in a hurry, "I'm just surprised. Amber and I went over the menu again last night and she seemed pretty set on it." I smiled apologetically.

He dialed his irritation down all the way from eleven to ten and a half. "She changed her mind. Shocking, I know. She wants to make those roasted vegetable things with the gravy."

I blinked. "The squash boats?"

"Whatever you made for Thanksgiving. Make that."

"The whole Thanksgiving menu?"

"Did I stutter?"

He strode out of the kitchen with Felix on his heels without waiting for my response, which was a good thing because once they were out of earshot I let loose a string of invective that would have made George Carlin roll over in his grave. I was still standing there in shock, trying to figure out how the devil I was supposed to pull off this switch on such short notice, when Alayna hurried by with a stack of freshly pressed linens in her arms.

She stopped and gaped at me in amazement. "Was that you I heard cursing?"

"Uh, yeah, sorry about that." I gave an embarrassed half-laugh and tried to arrange my face into a serene and spiritual expression befitting a holistic chef. I apparently failed because her concern only increased.

"Are you okay?" She scanned the counter, probably looking for a detached finger or a spider crawling in the fruit bowl. Something to explain the meltdown.

"Amber decided to make some last-minute adjustments to the menu," I explained, adopting the breeziest tone I could muster. "As in, she scrapped the whole thing, and I'm starting over with a new one."

Her eyes widened and she looked down in horror at the mountain of celadon green tablecloths and napkins she'd spent her morning ironing. "Oh, for the love of ... Please tell me she didn't change her color scheme."

I wish I could ease her mind, but this was our nightmare to share. "I have no idea. I'm sorry. You should ask her."

Alayna threw me a look that said 'yeah, I'll get right on that' and raced off in the direction of the dining room, clutching the linens to her chest and muttering in rapid-fire Spanish. I guess her plan was to hurry up and get the tables set, as if that would prevent Amber from changing her mind.

I really couldn't believe what Amber had done. Who goes from a tapas-based menu to a formal sit-down meal for forty people on the morning of the event? A vapid, self-absorbed twit, that's who. I had half a mind to track her down and try to convince her to stick with the original menu, but a glance at the iPad displaying her schedule revealed she had a busy day of primping ahead.

Besides, I really didn't have time to corner her between her facial and her manicure to plead what I knew would be a futile case. Amber wanted what Amber wanted. And she always got it. It was as simple as that. I set aside the eggplant, returned to the iPad to pull up the shopping list I'd used for the Patricks' Thanksgiving dinner, and started multiplying all the quantities by ten. My stomach growled to let me know it was time to sneak out for my fast food fix.

Forget the burger. I needed one of Pat's gin rickeys.

Three

I T WAS WELL AFTER MIDNIGHT when I tiptoed out of the kitchen with the last armload of picked-at food and eased the door shut with my hip. I waited until I heard the soft beep of the security system arming itself and then carefully made my way through the darkness to my car.

I was bent over the trunk, nesting the tray of stuffed squash into a spot next to the row of thermoses full of gravy when I heard gravel crunching behind me. I almost screamed but stopped myself in time. I slowly stood up, squeezed my eyes shut, and waited for the serial killer who was obviously skulking around behind me to strike.

When I was still alive a moment later, I forced myself to open my eyes and turn around. I found myself staring straight into the shining eyes of Antonio Santos, reputed Italian playboy, professional racecar driver, and next-door neighbor to the Patricks. By next-door neighbor, I mean owner of the distant mansion further down the private canyon drive, but you get the idea.

I'd seen him zooming by in his Bugatti Veyron every so often, usually with a dark-haired beauty in the passenger seat, but it's not like he ever knocked on the door to borrow a cup of sugar or the weed whacker or anything. So it wasn't immediately clear to me why he was standing in the driveway with a finger to his lips.

"You scared me," I said.

"My apologies." He gave me a smoldering look, which I immediately recognized from his photograph plastered all over the billboards hawking his macho body spray, Speed Demon.

"Uh, no problem. Can I help you with something?" I looked around but didn't see a car. Had he *walked* up the winding canyon road?

"No, no. I just ... I'm meeting someone," he said in a hushed, confidential tone.

Good for Alayna.

I tried to hide my smirk. "Okay, well I have to go."

I glanced at my watch. I had until one a.m. to get the food to the Loving Hands shelter before they lock the doors for the night. If I timed it right, I could hit the In-

N-Out Burger on my way home. The thought of a greasy sack of fries and a burger got my mouth watering and put a spring in my tired step.

I left the Latin lover standing in the driveway and peeled out like I was driving one of his cars and not a nine-year-old Saab.

~ ~ ~ ~ ~ ~ ~ ~ ~ ~

I groaned and smashed my pillow over my head in an attempt to block out the incessant hammering coming from the hallway. It was no use, though. The dull *thud, thud, thud* had penetrated my brain. I was fully awake now—and not too happy about it.

I threw off my light blanket and stomped toward the door to confront whomever had decided to embark on a home improvement project at seven o'clock on a Saturday morning. I caught a glimpse of myself in the foyer mirror, and let's just say I looked like a woman who'd spent the night in a homeless shelter.

Instead of dropping off the party leftovers and making a run for my long-delayed fast food, I'd somehow been suckered by Deb, the pink-haired angel who ran Loving Hands' perpetually understaffed kitchen, into peeling potatoes and making breakfast casseroles until the sun came up. Which had been about ninety minutes ago.

It wasn't until I was wrenching open my apartment door, that I realize the hammering sound was actually some jackass pounding on my door. My planned diatribe was cut short when I saw the trio on my doorstep. I could feel my mouth hanging open, so I clamped it shut and passed a hand through my wild bedhead. A young guy in a dark suit, my apologetic-looking building super, Mr. Rizzo, and an intense, middle-aged women buzzing with aggression looked back at me. The woman stepped forward.

"Are you Rosemary Field?" She asked in a clipped voice that matched her all-business pantsuit.

"Yes."

"I'm Detective Sullivan. This is Detective Drum-mond. May we come in?" She flashed her badge and was already halfway through the doorway when she asked the question. Her demeanor left no doubt that she was in charge.

My parents, card-carrying members of the ACLU that they were, had always taught my sisters and me not to invite law enforcement personnel into our private space. But then they turned out to have questionable judgment.

"Uh, sure, I guess."

Mr. Rizzo backed away and drifted down the hallway, while the male detective followed Detective Sullivan through the doorway and closed the door behind him. I glanced down at my filmy nightgown and crossed my arms over my chest.

"Sorry to have woken you, ma'am," Detective Drummond said. He gave me a boyish smile that I chose to believe was encouraging and not leering.

"It's okay. Can I throw on some clothes?" I asked. My mind raced as I tried to figure out what would bring these two to my door. I sincerely hoped it was to personally inform me that my deadbeat parents had been apprehended by the taxing authorities in some jurisdiction that still had debtors' prisons.

"That's a good idea, Ms. Field," Detective Sullivan said. "You don't mind if we have a look around while you get dressed, do you?"

"What's this about?" I didn't have anything to hide— except that jar of chocolate frosting with the spoon stuck in it, which comprised the sole contents of my refrigerator—but I didn't want anyone poking through my stuff, let alone the cops.

Detective Sullivan frowned, and I half-expected her to shout, 'I'll ask the questions here!' as if we were on the set of a crime drama.

Young Detective Drummond must have been assigned the role of good cop because he glanced at her then said in a mild tone, "We have some questions about a crime that occurred last night."

A crime?

"Did something happen at Loving Hands?" I asked.

He cocked his head at me. "The shelter on Inglewood?"

"That's the one."

"Why would you think we're here to ask you questions about a homeless shelter?" He screwed up his face in confusion.

"Well, that's where I was last night. I thought maybe someone broke into Deb's car or something. I mean, I don't know—*you're* the police." I looked pointedly at the little notebook he'd whipped out of his pocket.

"That's right. We are," Detective Sullivan said, seizing the opportunity to jump in and wrest back control of the conversation. "So go get decent and we can talk about what you know about the murder of Amber Patrick."

Everything slowed down, way down, it was like a super slow-mo scene from a cartoon. Her words echoed distortedly. My hand made its way up to cover my mouth as if it were cutting through pounds of molasses. "Amber's ... Dead? What happened?" My legs were trembling, so I leaned against the wall to avoid giving the authorities a real show by falling over on my ass clad in nothing but my short nightie.

"She ate your cooking," the detective cracked.

My eyes flew to the junior detective. "What's she talking about?"

"Mrs. Patrick died from anaphylactic shock," he said gently.

"What? She was fine when I left."

I mean, I assume she was fine. She'd taken a bottle of wine from the server, said good night, and made her way up the stairs to her bedroom while Alayna and I were cleaning up the kitchen. The last time I'd seen her, she'd been a little unsteady on her feet but definitely alive.

"The autopsy hasn't been completed, but the preliminary report is that she showed symptoms consistent with anaphylaxis at approximately oh one hundred hours and collapsed before Mr. Patrick could administer epinephrine," Detective Drummond explained.

I shook my head. Everything in my field of vision became wavy, like I was looking through water. "I don't understand."

"Let me make it simple, then. You were advised when you began working for Mrs. Patrick that she has an allergy to tree nuts and shellfish, were you not?" Detective Sullivan snapped.

"Of course." I answered numbly. I vaguely realized that I shouldn't even be talking to her but I didn't seem to be able to stop myself.

"And last night, you served your so-called famous vegan gravy, did you not?"

"Yes."

"A search of the recipe database on the iPad in the Patricks' kitchen showed that one of the ingredients in that gravy is cashews."

"It is," I agreed. "But I omit the nuts when I make it for Amber."

"Apparently you didn't this time," she countered.

"I did so. I doubled the oatmeal and added some extra mushrooms," I insisted.

Detective Drummond gave me a kind, almost apologetic, look. "We found the container of cashews in the trash in the kitchen, Ms. Field. You should put some clothes on. We're going to take a ride downtown."

Four

I WAS COUNTING THE CRACKS in the pea-soup green paint that coated the walls of the interview room in an effort to stave off a panic attack when the heavy metal door swung open.

I hoped against hope that Amber herself would come sashaying into the room, babbling an explanation about trying out a method acting technique or starring in an episode of some show like "Punk'd," but no such luck. Detective Drummond stood in the doorway and looked at me with sad, downcast eyes.

"I hope you're here to tell me that my lawyer's arrived," I said with bravado that I certainly didn't feel.

He didn't answer right away, just kept staring at me with an unreadable expression. I caught myself about to squirm in my seat and stilled my body. Was this some sort of interview technique intended to leverage the discomfort so many people seem to have with silence? If so, Detective Drummond was in for a surprise. I'd attended at least a half dozen silent meditation retreats at monasteries and yoga centers growing up. I mean, I'd gone ten days without speaking to my fellow spiritual pilgrims as a thirteen-year-old girl. I wasn't about to crack under the pressure of an uncomfortable pause. I pasted a beatific smile on my face and stared back at him.

After about ninety seconds, he blinked and then answered. "No, no lawyer. But your boyfriend's out front kicking up a fuss, throwing his weight around."

I opened my mouth to inform him that I didn't have a boyfriend but then thought the better of it. Maybe Deb hadn't been able to get a hold of the legal aid attorney who helped out at the shelter. Maybe she'd sent the janitor or one of the regulars down to pose as my boyfriend and ... and do exactly what, I wasn't sure. I hadn't been charged with anything (yet), so it wasn't like anyone could bail me out—at least, I didn't think so, based solely on my steady diet of police dramas on Netflix.

The police officer kept talking. "Sullivan sent me back here to cut you loose before the kid makes good on his promise to call the mayor at home on a Saturday morning." He shook his head. "Must be some kind of hot and heavy relationship if he's down here springing you instead of home mourning the loss of his stepmother."

My overwhelmed brain struggled to make sense of the words he was saying. *Felix* had come to rescue me? In my confusion, I forgot that I wasn't volunteering any information and said, "Felix and Amber weren't what you'd call close." As soon as the words popped out of my mouth, I wished I could grab them and shove them back in. But it was too late.

Interest sparked in Detective Drummond's eyes. "Oh, really? How 'not close' were they?"

'Not close' enough that he called her a whore yesterday, I thought. What I said was, "I really don't know."

He shook his head as if he were disappointed in me. He dropped the subject, though, and made a motion to usher me toward the door. As I walked past him, he asked in an offhand manner, "Hey, what made you decide to plan a formal sit-down dinner for last night's meal? Vegan turkey with all the trimmings? Seems like an odd choice, considering Thanksgiving was months ago."

I turned back to meet his eye. I was willing to stay silent about Felix's simmering hatred for his stepmother, but I couldn't let this guy impugn my professional reputation—or what was left of it in the aftermath of my client dying, apparently as a result of my cooking. He was looking at me with what appeared to be mild curiosity and genuine interest.

"I didn't. Yesterday morning, Amber changed my seasonal tapas menu to Thanksgiving dinner for forty."

His eyebrows crawled up his forehead and the skin around his eyes crinkled as he considered this information. He morphed from casual foodie into intense police officer instantly. "Really? Did she say why?"

I thought back to the previous day. With all my prep work for the party and Amber's prep work for her body, there hadn't been an opportunity for me to speak to her before her guests began to arrive. In fact, I realized, she hadn't said a word to me until just before she'd tripped her way up the stairs at the end of the night. "No," I said slowly. "Actually, she didn't even tell me herself. She sent her husband to tell me."

I looked meaningfully toward the door. I could tell he was just itching to ask me all sorts of questions, but I wanted to get out there before Felix got bored waiting and left me to my own devices. The detective's cheek muscle twitched, and I could also tell that he was remembering the fact that Felix was throwing some sort of fit in his boss' office. He sighed then nodded his head in a short, serious motion and pushed the door open for me. He led me through the maze of dingy, narrow corridors until we reached the front reception area.

As we rounded the corner into the lobby, Felix must have heard the sharp clacking as Detective Drummond's dress shoes struck the scuffed-up tile because his head jerked up from his iPhone as if someone had pulled an invisible string. I found myself wondering if the highly polished shoes were standard issue. *I* sure wouldn't have wanted to chase a perp in them. But then I readily admit the best thing about being a chef is having a bulletproof excuse for wearing Crocs.

Felix pocketed the phone and rushed toward us. "Rosemary, are you okay?" he asked with a surprising amount of concern.

He grabbed me by my shoulders and hugged me close to his solid chest, and I noticed the following things: one, he smelled like bourbon; and two, Detective Drummond was shuffling his feet and staring fixedly at the wall.

"I'm fine," I said. I pulled back and searched his face. "I want you to know I didn't kill Amber. There weren't any nuts in that gravy."

He waved away the subject of his stepmother's death. "We can talk about it someplace else. Let's get you out of here."

He didn't need to ask me twice. Without so much as another glance at Detective Drummond, I started for the door.

As Felix pulled open the door, the detective called after us, "We'll be talking to you again soon, Ms. Field. In the meantime, don't make any plans to leave town."

~ ~ ~ ~ ~ ~ ~ ~ ~ ~

Felix didn't say anything as we walked through the parking lot toward his Porsche Boxster convertible, which I couldn't help but note was parked illegally in a fire zone.

"Really? At the police station?" I asked.

He just laughed at my disbelief and beeped his key fob to open the door. As we neared the car I noticed a parking ticket tucked under the driver's side windshield wiper. He saw it, too, and plucked it away. He stared right at me while he rolled the slip of paper into a ball and tossed it to the ground.

"Add littering to my list of heinous crimes, Rose-mary." He gave me a big grin.

Despite myself, I had to laugh. After the miserable morning I'd spent dealing with the cops, his trust fund baby antics amused rather than irritated me. My mood improved even further when he hurried around to the passenger side of the car and held open the door for me.

"Thanks." I settled myself back into the soft leather seats while he slid behind the wheel and revved the engine as if daring the police to come out and give him a ticket for anticipated speeding. I just shook my head. Then I had a thought. "Are you sure you're okay to drive?"

He shot me a look. "I'm fine. Why?"

"I thought I smelled booze on your breath."

"Oh. My dad and I were, uh, honoring Amber's memory."

Uh-huh. More like celebrating the fact that the wicked witch was dead. But I just nodded. "Oh."

"I had one drink, hours ago. Honest."

As he peeled out and merged into the traffic flowing by, I said, "Thank you for coming to get me."

He slipped a pair of sunglasses out of the visor and onto his face. "No thanks needed, Rosemary. You never should have been dragged down there in the first place, I know you didn't kill Amber."

I bit my lip, hesitating. Finally, I decided to go ahead and ask. "How can you be so sure? Do you know who did?"

He glanced over at me but I couldn't read his expression from behind his shades. The buttery leather suddenly felt hot and sticky against my back.

After a moment, he answered in a flat, emotionless tone. "No, I don't. But I'm sure it wasn't you. I've seen Amber berate you plenty of times. You never get upset by it. You never get upset by anything, and I don't think your equanimity is an act. I just think you're not that kind of person." He flashed a smile and returned his attention to the traffic ahead.

It was true. I did maintain my cool when Amber was ripping into me, and, while I wouldn't say it was an act, it certainly didn't come easy. I just couldn't afford to lose my job. As a result, I did more loving kindness meditation while working for a Hollywood actress than I'd ever done while living with my parents.

That thought made me realize for the first time that I *had* almost certainly just lost my job. The woman who had hired me was lying in the morgue. And I somehow doubted Pat and Felix were going to keep me around for my gluten-free pad thai. My stomach lurched and I thought I was going to redecorate the interior of Felix's sports car. I clamped my mouth shut and focused on my breathing until the moment passed.

Oblivious to the how close he'd come to a vomit-covered vehicle, he kept talking. "Are you hungry? I'm starving."

Was I hungry? As unbelievable as it might sound, after spending the morning at the police station refusing to answer questions about whether I killed my boss, and now facing the looming prospect of joblessness, I was famished.

"I guess I could eat a bite," I said in a noncommittal way, hoping that he was asking if I wanted to grab a lunch and not suggesting that I go back to the mansion and cook him something. Although the latter would suggest job security.

As it turned out, it was the former.

"Good. There's a fantastic *taqueria* right around the corner. You're gonna love it."

He hit the gas and cut off an SUV to make a left turn onto a side street at a rate of speed that I was certain was neither safe nor legal, tires squealing. My not-quite-settled stomach protested. We crawled along for another block, stop and go, stop and go, then he took another left and pulled into an uninspired strip mall. The taco joint was sandwiched between a dry cleaner and a garage. He found a spot in front of the garage and parked. I eyed the restaurant in disbelief. I realize he's a human being just like me, but it was impossible to picture Felix hunched over a melamine table eating a taco out of a plastic basket. I shouldn't have worried; as it turned out, he had other plans.

"This place is great," he assured me as we walked through the door.

At the jangle of bells announcing our arrival, the guy behind the counter raised his head and beamed. "Ah, Señor Patrick!"

"Miguel, how you doing, my man?" Felix said, reaching out to shake the man's hand.

"Good, good. You want your usual?"

"You know it."

"To go?"

"Of course."

Miguel eyed me with open curiosity. Even on my best day, I knew I didn't compare to the well-heeled Malibu Barbies Felix probably brought in here all the time. But on a day when I'd had almost no sleep and then been dragged out of bed at seven in the morning and hauled down to the police station? I have long, straight blonde hair, but that's where the California girl comparison ended. For one thing, my hair was piled in a messy knot on the top of my head. For another, I wasn't wearing any makeup to hide the dark smudges under my eyes. And to complete the picture, when Detective Drummond and his evil pal Detective Sullivan had told me to get dressed I'd grabbed the first clothes I'd found—a pair of slouchy gray sweatpants and a faded Duke tee shirt. In other words, I looked like fresh-buttered hell.

I smiled at him in the hopes that friendliness would make up for my appearance.

"And what will *la señorita bonita* have?" Miguel asked, returning my smile.

The pretty woman? Either this guy had extraordinary low standards or Felix was an outstanding tipper. I chuckled and scanned the menu board behind his head. "What's good?" I asked.

"Everything," he and Felix answered in unison.

"In that case, surprise me," I said, suddenly overwhelmed by the mere thought of choosing a meal. To my dismay, all the shock and stress of the day poured over me at once. I was a woman teetering on the verge of breaking down. *You just need something to eat,* I told myself. *Blood sugar's probably low.*

Miguel nodded as if accepting my challenge. "Good, good," he said as he bustled away.

Felix grinned down at me. I suddenly felt awkward being out for lunch with my dead boss' stepson. I searched my mind for a topic of conversation but came up empty. I was too drained to devise appropriate small talk, so I pretended to study the menu so as to avoid having to talk to Felix.

After a moment, the whirring of a commercial juicer saved me from having to even pretend to talk. It sounded like a jet taking off. After several loud minutes, the noise cut out. A moment later Miguel returned, bearing two large glasses. One was a bright orange color and the other was the lightest pink.

Only in Los Angeles, I thought, *would a taco stand double as a juice bar. Everywhere else in America, you get your tacos with a frosty Corona.*

"Here. Something to drink while you're waiting." Miguel handed the glasses over the counter. He thrust the orange one into my hands and handed the pink one to Felix.

I sniffed the vibrant liquid. "Carrots?" I guessed.

Miguel nodded. "With some lime juice, cilantro, and fresh ginger. It should pep you up. Late night, eh?" He flashed a knowing smile and glanced toward Felix.

I flushed. Not only was my exhaustion showing, but Miguel was making wild assumptions about its cause.

"What's his?" I said nodding my head toward Felix's juice.

"Oh, it's my usual," Felix answered quickly. "Apple pineapple."

"And a little chamomile and valerian," Miguel added.

I cocked my head. "If ginger and cilantro are for a pick-me-up, what're the chamomile and valerian for? Are you trying to calm him down?"

Miguel laughed, but Felix nodded. "Yeah, it helps me stay calm. I ... well ... I can have a bit of a quick temper at times," he said with a sheepish grin.

Tell me about it, I thought, recalling his little outburst in the kitchen yesterday morning, but I said nothing. Instead, I took a cautious sip of the carrot juice, not expecting much from a *taqueria* slash juice bar. It was surprisingly good.

"Mmm," I said, "Nice balance."

"Thanks," Miguel answered.

Felix chimed in. "You may not know what high praise that is. Rosemary is my family's private chef—a holistic chef." He drained his juice with one long, noisy swallow and slammed the glass on the counter as if he were at a bar throwing back shots.

I shook my head.

The phrase 'holistic chef' sparked Miguel's interest. "Oh yeah? Bet that's a nice gig. Did you go to culinary school?"

"Not exactly," I answered. I didn't know how much of my background Amber shared with Felix, but I really didn't feel like discussing my fall from the chemistry lab to his family's magazine-perfect kitchen. His stepmother had known from my résumé that I'd been a research scientist, but she hadn't been sufficiently interested to ask why I'd trade my career for a job waiting on her.

A timer sounded somewhere in the back. Miguel excused himself to go check on our food.

I turned to Felix and appraised him over my juice glass. "You said I *am* your family's private chef. Don't you mean I *was?*"

He furrowed his brow at me. "What do you mean by that?"

I didn't know if he was playing dumb or if the situation really hadn't occurred to him. I sipped my carrot juice and decided to give him the benefit of the doubt. "Well, Amber hired me. I didn't get the sense that you or your dad approved of most of her choices. I assume with Amber gone, so is my job."

Felix shook his head. "Nah, I don't think so, Rosemary. It's true that Amber wasn't exactly known for her great decision-making skills, but I think everyone in the house would agree that hiring you was one of the smartest things she ever did." He pierced me with a long, appreciative look, and my cheeks grew warm yet again.

"Oh," I stammered, "thank you."

He went on. "It's not like my dad and I are going to start cooking for ourselves now, and there's no way Alayna's going to agree to do it. So I'm sure my dad would say the job is yours as long as you still want it."

"I still want it," I said. Immediately a huge wave of relief crashed over me.

"Good," he said. A slow smile spread across his lips.

I turned my attention back to the juice and took another big drink. "This really is very good."

"Wait until you taste his cooking."

As if he'd been summoned by the mention of his food, Miguel returned carrying a large brown bag. The fragrant scent of fresh, hot Mexican food wafted toward me as he passed it to Felix. "You're all set. Utensils, plates, the works."

Felix pulled out his wallet and peeled off some twenties. "Thanks, Miguel."

"Thank you," I echoed, finishing my juice. I placed the empty glass next to Felix's.

"De nada," Miguel answered. He nodded toward me and added, "Rosemary, you come back and let me know what you think of my cooking, chef to chef." He put his head down and went back to chopping tomatoes and dicing jalapeños.

I trailed Felix out into the parking lot. The midday sun was bright overhead, and the heat undulated up from the pavement in waves. I blinked and lowered my gaze to the ground.

"No sunglasses? What kind of Angeleno are you?" he teased.

"I left my place at seven in the morning. I didn't think to grab a pair. I didn't even take my phone. I'm not used to getting a wake up call from the cops."

He nodded. "I bet that was really disorienting. And scary." His voice was soft. He sounded genuinely sympathetic, and, for some reason, the hint of tenderness almost made me cry.

We reached his car but he kept walking.

"What are you doing?" I asked, standing beside the Boxster.

"You'll see; it's a surprise. Come on. It's not far," he gestured with his arm to wave me forward.

I hesitated, chewing on my lower lip. I was in no mood for any more surprises. But I *was* about to faint from hunger. I started walking toward him, grumbling under my breath. He just laughed and, when I caught up with him, draped his arm around my shoulder casually. My bare arm tingled at the contact, so I grumbled a little louder to cover up my reaction.

Five

ESPITE MY WHEEDLING, Felix steadfastly refused to give me any hints during our short walk. His surprise turned out to be an amazing apartment just a few blocks away from the taco stand. He stopped in front of an ornate, wrought-iron gate and juggled the bag while he fished out a key from his pants pocket. He unlocked the gate and led me into a lush, flowering garden. I followed him, my jaw hanging open at the sight of the hundreds, maybe thousands, of blooming plants. I wandered off the stepping stone path to trail a finger along bougainvillea, tall lavender, enormous hydrangea, and fragrant roses. I spotted a patch of sage blossoming near purple sweet pea flowers. The path circled past a stone fountain, water tinkling gently, and a butterfly garden then poured us out onto a patio where a small table and two chairs sat, shaded from the blazing sun by a khaki canvas umbrella.

Felix anticipated my question and answered it before I could ask it. "Our recording studio keeps this apartment for vocalists and musicians who travel in from out of town."

I nodded, unable to find words to do justice to the stunning garden. "Wow," I finally managed.

He laughed and deposited our lunch on the table. Then he frowned as he noticed the place settings and crystal pitcher of ice water, lemon slices floating on the surface.

"Did you plan this?" I asked, even though I suspected, based on his bewildered expression, that he hadn't.

"No," he answered slowly, wrinkling his brow. "We have a service that takes care of our visitors; they must've gotten confused. No one's staying here now." After a moment, he shrugged and started dishing out the food. He piled fresh guacamole, housemade salsa, and tender *carne asada* on our plates and set the little covered dish of tortillas in the center of the table.

The scent of flowers in bloom permeated the walled garden. Unseen birds sang in the lemon and avocado trees that lined the path. Between the food and the setting, it was as close to paradise as a girl could get within the city limits. The grim holding room in the police station seemed like it was in another country, not around the corner.

"This place is amazing," I said as I tucked my napkin into my lap. It truly was—in some ways, it reminded me of my parents' resort.

Felix nodded around a mouthful of shredded pork. "I always thought of this as my own little oasis. I like to come here sometimes just to get away from Amber and my dad. I used to, I mean," he added.

At the mention of his dead stepmother, reality came rushing back, undoing all of the tranquility provided by the surroundings. "I can't believe she's dead," I said lamely.

He watched me scoop some guacamole onto the chip. Then he swallowed and said, "Yeah. Obviously, she wasn't my favorite person. But I can't believe someone actually killed her. You know?"

"Not just killed her. Somebody killed her *and* framed me." Saying the words aloud destroyed my appetite and I rested my fork against the side of my plate.

Felix's eyes were full of concern. He stared hard at me across the table. "Listen, Rosemary, I promise we'll figure this out. I don't want you to stress about this. Okay?"

I wanted to believe him, so I nodded and pushed down the panic that was bubbling up in my chest. "How's your dad taking it?" I asked mainly to distract myself, not out of any great concern about Pat's mental state.

He shrugged. "Okay, I suppose. I'm not sure why he married her in the first place to be honest. They sure as hell were never in love." He returned his attention to his taco.

"Maybe he married her to give you a stepmother?" I asked delicately. I didn't know much about Amber and Pat's relationship, but I could see a father wanting his son to have a maternal presence in his life.

"I hope not." He laughed bitterly and explained, "I was almost twenty when he married her, so that ship had pretty well sailed. Plus, don't forget, she was only three years older than me. She wasn't some kind of substitute mom. My dad raised me on his own. I never even knew my actual mom. She split when I was a newborn. So, it was always just 'the Patrick guys.'" He stabbed at a stray hunk of meat, spearing it with his fork. "Then all of a sudden, Amber shows up. I come home from college one weekend and there she is, prancing around the kitchen like she's in the Victoria's Secret fashion show."

"I'm sorry." I didn't know what else to say.

"Don't be. I figured my dad was looking for a good time, and, you know, he's entitled to it. He always told me not to count on inheriting his fortune. I figured he planned to blow it on Amber, which was fine with me—until I got to know her."

I reached for my glass and took a long drink to avoid having to respond substantively to that.

He rolled along, undaunted by my silence. "Amber was cheating on my dad."

My eyebrows crawled up my forehead, and, before I could stop myself, I asked, "How do you know?"

"I overheard her taunting him. He was on his way to the gym to work out and she said something along the lines of 'keep trying; maybe if you work at it long enough you can look half as good as my lover.'"

Not to speak ill of the newly dead, but that was just the sort of cutting, caustic remark that Amber was famous for. Well, actually, Amber was famous for her all-American charm and brilliant smile. But those of us whose exposure went beyond her peppy interviews on "Entertainment Tonight" knew that her nasty wit was her predominant characteristic.

"I'm sorry," I mumbled. I desperately wanted to ask who she'd been sleeping with, but that was too far across the line, so I bit down on my lip and told myself to be polite.

He seemed to guess what I was thinking. "I don't know who she was talking about—I don't even know if she limited herself to just one. But don't be sorry, it's just the way she was. My dad had to know what he was getting into when he asked that witch to marry him." His tone was bitter.

My eyes widened and it occurred to me that if he kept making comments along those lines it would put neither him nor his dad in the best light with the police. I considered pointing that out, but then it also dawned on me that, as the current primary suspect, it wouldn't hurt me if the police decided to look a little closer at the Patrick family. A small twinge of guilt plucked at me, but self-preservation won out, and I kept my mouth clamped firmly shut.

Felix seemed to misinterpret my silent struggle with my conscience as a bout of shock or offense of some sort. He gave me a pitying look and said, "I'm sure this all sounds crazy to you. I imagine you had a totally normal childhood with the white picket fence and all that," he remarked.

I nearly choked on my tortilla chip. If he only knew. My childhood was about as far from the typical American upbringing as a person could get outside of Hollywood, but the last thing I felt like doing was telling Felix all about my crazy family.

My family. Crap!

"My sister!" I exclaimed, standing up and nearly upending the table in my panic. "I just remembered my sister's in town this weekend. She's probably frantic. I left with the cops in such a hurry, I didn't even grab my phone."

He stood. "It's okay, take it easy. Here, call her and let her know you're on your way." He handed me his phone.

I stared down at it and realized I didn't actually know Sage's cell phone number anymore. I'd become so dependent on my contacts list, I couldn't have called her if I'd wanted to. I met his eyes with a helpless look. "I don't have her number memorized."

"Okay, hey no worries. We'll get you home in no time."

His put a hand on my shoulder and started guiding me toward the gate.

"What about this mess?" I asked, glancing behind me at the half-eaten meal we'd left behind.

"I'll call the service. Come on."

We jogged all the way back to his car.

Six

ON AN ORDINARY DAY—that is, one where I wasn't freaking out about leaving my sister (and possibly two little kids) hanging and worrying about being charged for my boss' murder—I would have spent the hair-raising car ride from the taco shop to my apartment alternating between musing about whether Felix was romantically interested in me and offering up prayers that we didn't die in a fiery crash, as his speedometer inched closer and closer to triple digits. But, as things stood, I was glad that he drove with no regard for the law or our personal safety. I was so panicked about Sage that I had my seatbelt unbuckled and was halfway out of my seat by the time he squealed to a stop in front of my building.

"Thanks!" I shouted over my shoulder, as I sprinted up the stairs. It wasn't until I was jiggling my key in the temperamental front door lock that I processed the fact that he'd been leaning across the front seat, his eyes closed, when I leapt from the car.

He was moving in to kiss you, you idiot.

I turned and shot him a look over my shoulder, mortified by the prospect that I'd offended him without even realizing it. He didn't look put out. Instead, if anything, he looked moderately amused. He draped his right arm over the back of the empty passenger seat, gave me a short *beep* and a broad smile, then zoomed out into traffic.

I shoved thoughts of Felix out of my mind and raced up to the fourth floor, taking the stairs two at a time. I pushed open the heavy fire door and burst into the hallway, panting. I'd planned to sprint down the hall to my apartment and grab my phone to call Sage, but when I saw the crowd assembled in front of my door I drew up short.

A frazzled-looking Sage, two small, tanned, and towheaded beauties with enormous blue eyes, and Detective Drummond all stared at me.

"Rosemary," Sage practically shouted, "where have you *been?!*" She loped down the hall and half-tackled, half-hugged me.

I squeezed her back, tightly, and inhaled the gingery scent of whatever shampoo she was using on her bouncy, copper-colored hair. "Sage, you wouldn't believe the day I've had," I whispered.

She pulled back and gripped my arms, piercing me with a look. "I heard some of it. Amber Patrick's been murdered?" she said in a hushed voice.

"Yeah, and Captain America over there thinks I did it," I whispered, cutting my eyes toward Detective Drummond, who appeared to be deeply engaged in a rousing game of paddy cake with Skylar, while Dylan looked on, rapt.

Sage shook her head. "Detective Drummond? No, I don't think he does. He seems like a good guy. But his boss ..." she trailed off and started gnawing on a ragged cuticle with her teeth.

I slapped her hand lightly and pulled her finger out of her mouth. "Stop that."

Detective Drummond raised his head and met my gaze. "Where's your boyfriend?"

I could feel Sage eying me curiously. I took a deep breath and exhaled then said, "Felix Patrick isn't my boyfriend."

The police officer raised a skeptical eyebrow. "Really? Someone ought to let him know."

"Felix?" Sage murmured beside me. "Have you been holding out on me?"

I huffed. "No," I said out of the side of my mouth. Then I turned my attention back to LAPD's finest. "He's a friend. Or maybe he's just a concerned citizen who objects to the way your department seems to be hell-bent on railroading me. Anyway, what are you doing here? Were you hoping to break in and execute an illegal, warrantless search while I wasn't home?" My voice sounded stiff and angry even to me.

Great, Rosemary, make him think you have a bad temper. That'll help your situation.

Beside me, Sage sort of muttered under her breath. I couldn't make out the words, but I got the impression that she also may have thought my jab was ill-advised.

I ignored the anger flashing in Detective Drummond's eyes and walked over to crouch in front of the kids. "You must be Dylan," I said to the boy.

"Yes, ma'am," he said in a shy voice.

"And I'm Skylar!" his sister piped up.

"Hi, Skylar." I looked from one round little face to the other. "My name's Rosemary. I'm Sage's big sister."

"We know," Skylar informed me seriously.

"Are you a bad guy?" Dylan wanted to know.

I glared at Detective Drummond as if to say 'see what you've done?' He matched my gaze with a calm, impassive look. I was surprised to note that his brown eyes were flecked with gold. What he said next was even more surprising.

He took Dylan's hands in his own and said, "Now listen up. This is important. In this country, no one is bad guy until a judge and a jury say so. Understand? And your nanny's sister, I don't think a judge and jury will ever say she's a bad guy. I think she might just be mixed up in something she doesn't quite understand."

Dylan nodded solemnly.

Skylar considered this information then turned to Detective Drummond and asked, "So are you here to help her?"

"If she'll let me," he told her.

Sage had come over to stand beside me. She arched her brow and gave me a look that suggested she believed him. I bet she'd feel somewhat less charitably toward the good officer if he'd dragged *her* out of bed and down to the police station for a fun morning of being treated like a criminal. But I held my tongue. And, if I'm being honest, the solemn, serious way he addressed the kids' worries melted my heart just the teensiest bit.

I stood and motioned for Detective Drummond to do the same. He gave the kids one final reassuring smile and then rose to his feet.

"If that's true, I guess I should apologize for my crack about the warrantless search," I said in a magnanimous tone.

He nodded.

I smiled. *Good; I'm glad that's out of the way,* I thought.

"Go ahead," he said.

"Go ahead?" I echoed.

"Go ahead and apologize," he told me, catching me in the same behavior I'd called Felix on less than twenty-four hours earlier. Detective Drummond pursed his lips and tried to hide his amusement.

I didn't bother to hide mine. I threw back my head and laughed then said, "Well played. Let me clarify. I'm sorry for the crack about the illegal search. And I would really appreciate some help."

His lips curved into a genuine smile. "Good. Take care of your visitors and then we'll talk."

~ ~ ~ ~ ~ ~ ~ ~ ~ ~

It took me what seemed like forever to convince Sage to leave—she was worried about me, afraid to leave me alone. Finally, I promised to meet her and the kids at the Santa Monica Pier and to keep my phone charged and handy then shoved her and the two blonde cuties out of the building. I hustled Detective Drummond into my apartment and headed for the kitchen.

"I need some tea," I told him as I plugged in the electric kettle. "You interested?"

"You have loose tea and milk?" he asked in return.

"No milk," I said, recalling the sad state of my fridge. "Why?"

"I can make a mean chai."

I shot him a disbelieving look over my shoulder.

"What?" he said.

"You don't look like the chai type."

"Chai's a type?"

"Whatever. You just strike me as more of a black coffee kind of guy," I said.

He let that go. Instead he said, "Sure, I'd love some tea. So, Sage is your older sister?"

I dug around in the cabinet and found the little wooden chest of fancy teas I'd liberated from the kitchen at my parent's resort. As I placed the selection of teas on the wobbly IKEA table, I gave him a questioning glance. "No, I'm the oldest. Why?"

"She seems very maternal, the way she was clucking over you. I figured she was used to taking care of you." He shrugged and flipped through the tea packets, settling on a hot pepper/mint/green tea combination.

I plucked a vanilla chamomile packet out of the pile and tore it open. "No. I'm the oldest. Sage is in the middle. And our baby sister is Thyme." I waited for the stupid joke, but it never came. I blinked. Sage had once informed me that she'd spent three months keeping count: upon hearing our names, eighty-seven percent of men and seventy-two percent of women responded with a lame crack. What she expected me to do with this information, I'd never known, but I figured that's just the way accountants' brains work.

"Huh. Well your younger sister sure is concerned about you," he observed.

The kettle beeped to let me know the water was hot. I sort of missed the whistle of a stovetop kettle, but convenience trumps nostalgia. I grabbed two mugs from the cabinet overhead and plunked them down on the counter. "Of course she is. You're trying to pin a murder on me." I turned to face him.

He held up his hands in a gesture of appeasement. "Listen. What I said to those kids is true. I don't think you killed Amber Patrick. But I *do* think you know more than you're letting on about her death. And, yes, someone's gone through a fair amount of trouble to make it look like you killed her. So, what we need to figure out together is who and why."

I clamped my lips together and crossed my arms.

He took in my defensive posture for a moment and then shrugged. "It's your move, Rosemary. Detective Sullivan's in a hurry to clear this and get the freaking paparazzi out of her hair. If I don't give her another viable suspect, she'll do exactly that and move on with her life."

I sighed but softened my stance—literally and figuratively. "What exactly do you want to know?" I sighed as I poured the hot water into the mugs and passed him one so he could steep his teabag.

I watched with a mixture of horror and fascination as Detective Drummond dumped a metric buttload of sugar from the sugar bowl on the table into his mug.

"Who else knew about her food allergies? And had access to the kitchen? And had a reason to want to kill her?" he asked, shoveling still more sugar into his tea.

I was still staring at the sugar bowl. The thought of drinking the mess in his mug made my teeth ache.

"Rosemary?" he prompted.

I shook my head. "Sorry. I got distracted there watching you fixing your tea." I dragged my eyes away from the sugar bomb in his hands.

He reddened. "I'm a southern boy. I do like a sweet tea," he admitted.

"You don't say? But I don't hear an accent."

"I've been out here for a long time, since right after high school. It only kicks back in when I'm back home. Anyway—means, motive, opportunity? Any thoughts?"

I stirred my tea and thought about his questions. "Well, everybody knew about her nut allergy."

"How?"

I lowered myself into the chair across from him. My kitchen table was so tiny that our knees touched underneath. He discreetly scooted his chair back—and banged directly into the oven. "Tight quarters," I said with an apologetic smile before answering his question. "Amber made it a point to educate everyone who came into the house as to her food allergies, sensitivities, and preferences."

"What exactly do you mean by 'everyone'?"

"I mean she wanted to make sure that nobody introduced any products that contained nuts or wheat, among other verboten items, into her environment in any capacity. That included her massage therapist, her hairstylist, the maid, and, of course, me. Not only did she not want to eat any nuts, she didn't want to touch anything that had been remotely near a nut."

"Was her allergy that severe?" he asked.

I entertained the thought of making the obvious joke that she was nuts but decided not to pick that low-hanging fruit. "I honestly don't know. It could've been. Or she could have simply been being overly dramatic about it because she was overly dramatic about pretty much everything." Subtlety hadn't been Amber's forte.

"It sounds like you didn't like your boss very much," he remarked.

Despite the fact that his tone was nonjudgmental, even gentle, I stiffened. "She was a hard person to like," I finally said, cringing at how defensive I sounded.

"Oh?"

"Yeah. She was mean to the people who worked for her, dismissive of the people who she worked with, difficult toward the people who she worked for, and generally only turned on her pleasant persona when the cameras were rolling and she was being paid to be charming."

"Why didn't you quit?"

No way was I getting into *that* whole mess with the LAPD. "I need the money," I said in a flat voice that left no doubt the topic was off-limits.

He raised an eyebrow but moved on without prodding. "So would you say she had a lot of *enemies?*"

"I don't know about enemies, but there certainly were a lot of people who had their differences with her."

"What about her relationship with her husband?" he pressed, taking a great, big gulp of his tea.

"What about it?" I stalled as I considered how to answer the question in a way that was at least fair to Pat, who apparently was going to continuing employing me.

He leaned forward with interest and our knees bumped again. "Sorry," he mumbled.

I waved off the apology and said slowly, "I heard she was openly carrying on an affair, so I wouldn't rate it as a great relationship."

"Did they fight a lot?" he asked.

I thought he'd be more interested in the affair, but he was the law enforcement expert—maybe it's never the lover. "Like I said, she was generally nasty. She fought with Pat, sure, but she fought with everyone."

"Does that include your *friend* Felix?"

I ignored the sarcastic emphasis on Felix's name and answered the question honestly. "Yes. I don't think Felix got along any better with Amber than did the rest of us."

"Hmm. Okay, back to the bit about the boyfriend "

"I told you he's not my boyfriend," I snapped, cutting him off.

He reached for his tea and gave me a lazy smile. "Methinks the lady doth protest too much. I wasn't asking about your boyfriend, I was asking about Amber's boyfriend."

I took a drink of my own tea to cover my embarrassed discomfort. I was about to confess that all I knew about Amber's purported affair had come from Felix when the image of the swarthy Italian playboy next door popped into my head. "Well it's an open secret that Amber's cheating on Pat, apparently. And last night, when I was leaving to get in my car to go home, one of the neighbors was lurking around the house. He scared me half to death."

"When was this?"

"It had to be almost one in the morning."

"Who was it?"

"Antonio Santos. You know, the racecar driver?"

"The Eurotrash playboy who hawks the stinky body wash?"

"That's the one."

"And it didn't occur to you to mention this little tidbit to me and Detective Sullivan this morning?" he exploded, his voice vibrating with barely contained anger.

"I honestly didn't think of it until just now. I've had a sort of disorienting day," I said pointedly.

He had the decency not to argue the point. "What happened with Santos?"

"Like I said, he startled me. He said he was meeting someone."

"Did he say who?" Detective Drummond asked. He drained his mug and returned it to the table with a thud.

"No, he didn't. At the time, I sort of thought he was meeting another one of the household staff members, but now I wonder. Maybe he was there for Amber."

I could see him weighing that possibility. Given Santos' reputation, it certainly seemed plausible to me.

"You think he killed her?"

"I have no idea. Maybe? Or maybe Pat had had enough of her adultery." I shrugged. As much as I wanted the police to move away from the notion that I'd killed Amber, I wasn't comfortable offering up another juicy suspect. They could do their own legwork.

He eyed me closely. "Is there anything else you forgot to tell us this morning?"

I gnawed on my lower lip, hesitating. I didn't want to be the one to tell the investigators about Felix's outburst, but I didn't want Detective Drummond to find out from someone else and think I was holding out on him. I needed this guy to help me. After a moment, I exhaled slowly and said, "Well, there is one other thing. It's probably nothing ..."

"What is it?" he said in a tone that suggested he was irritated, but not surprised, to learn that there was more I hadn't told him.

"Yesterday morning, I was talking to Felix and I referred to Amber as his mother. He got pretty mad, and I corrected myself to say she was his stepmother ... and ... he kind of stomped off. Later, he apologized but then he called her a whore." I finished speaking and lowered my eyes, feeling more horrible by the minute about the fact that I was probably putting Felix in the same terrible spot I was in.

Detective Drummond was silent for so long that I couldn't stand it and started to yammer again. "I mean, I don't think he killed her or anything. I just thought I should make sure you heard it from me. He didn't like her, but then again—"

"I know," he interrupted, "no one liked her."

"It's true." I protested. I was worried he thought I was making excuses for Felix now. This dealing with the police business was nerve racking.

He looked at me closely, "it may be true, but that's not going to help you. If I report back that everyone who ever met Amber would have a motive to kill her, Detective Sullivan's just going to double down on the suspect we've already identified as also having means and opportunity. That would be you."

I stared into my tea, wishing that I could read my future in the leaves. Finally, I raised my head and met his unblinking eyes. "I honestly don't know what to say. I want your help but I don't think I have any better information. If I were you, I'd start with Antonio Santos."

He locked eyes with me, and I could see the worry clouding his expression.

Great. If he's worried, I should be in a full-on panic.

He cleared his throat and stood up, slipping back into his formal police officer voice. "Thank you for talking with me, ma'am."

We're back to ma'am? It's even worse than I thought.

I walked him to the door. Before I opened it, I said, "Thank you for believing me. I didn't kill her."

He gave me a sad smile. "I know." A heavy silence followed. I could tell he was thinking the same thing I was—unless he figured out who did, it wasn't going to matter whether he believed me or not. I'd be charged with murder. He stepped out into the hallway and closed the door behind him, leaving me alone with my dark thoughts.

Seven

"I'M REALLY SORRY ABOUT ALL THIS," I said to Sage.

We were sitting on a bench in the hippodrome, watching Skylar and Dylan spin by on the old-fashioned carousel in giddy circles. Even over the music, I could hear them shrieking with laughter.

"What are you sorry about? Being framed for murder? I agree, it's really poor hostess form to get hauled to the clink when your sister's visiting from the other side of the country." Sage rolled her eyes.

"Don't be a brat. I'm sorry that you didn't get to meet Amber. Sorry that I can't hang out with you more. And very sorry that you got stuck in the hallway with Detective Crankypants."

She shook her head at me, making her coppery curls bob and dance against her bare shoulders. "Dave? He wasn't cranky. He's a good guy."

"Dave? Who the—wait, Detective Drummond? He told you to call him *Dave?*"

"Why wouldn't he? I'm not the one he's investigating for killing her boss."

"Point taken."

We sat in silence for a few rotations of the painted horses. Then she said, "So where were you anyway? Dave—Detective Drummond, I mean—said, uh, Felix picked you up at the station?"

I flushed. "He did. It was ... weird. He came down and harangued the detective in charge until she sprung me. And then he took me to lunch."

"Like a date?"

Was it a date? I had no flipping idea. It had sort of felt like one. But who put the moves on his stepmother's suspected killer? And it had seemed like he was going to kiss me there at the end.

"Not exactly," I finally said.

Sage looked unconvinced. "Hmm. Well, I guess it's good he got you out. He obviously doesn't think you killed Amber."

"Yeah, he doesn't. But I'm not sure he'd care if I had killed her. He kind of hated her."

She paused to wave at the kids as they circled past. Then she asked the money question. "Did he hate her enough to kill her?"

"No. I don't think so. He said she was having an affair, though. I think I ran into her boyfriend last night outside the house."

Interest sparked in her eyes. *Uh-oh.* I recognized that expression. Thyme and I called it her Lucille Ball look.

"Hey —"

"Whatever screwball idea you're about to propose, the answer is 'no,'" I interrupted her in my best oldest sister voice.

"Rude. You don't even know what I was going to say."

"I bet I can guess. It involves some sort of dangerous, madcap behavior."

"You're so wrong."

"Really?" I doubted it.

"All I was going to say was we should follow him," she said.

"We? As in me, you, and two little kids? And him? As in ... the guy Amber was cheating on her husband with? The guy who might have killed her? Yeah, you're right. That's not irresponsible and risky—not at all."

She pouted for a second. Then she sighed. "I guess you're right. I can't trail the guy. *I* have responsibilities." She cut her eyes meaningfully toward the merry-go-round. As if on cue, the music died and the ride slowed to a stop. She stood.

"You aren't really suggesting that I should try to keep tabs on a professional race car driver, are you? Do you plan to pay my speeding tickets?"

She glanced at me. "He's a race car driver?"

"Antonio Santos."

"Wow. You're so glamorous. You know him, too?"

"Not exactly," I assured her.

"Huh. Well, since you're possibly the most cautious driver I've ever met, you're not the best candidate for this mission anyway. Maybe you should leave it to Detective Dave."

Skylar and Dylan came racing toward us, still laughing.

"Can we get an ice cream, Sage? Please?" Dylan asked.

"Sure. Ice cream cones for everyone. And then we'll hit the aquarium. Rosemary says it's really cool." She grinned as the kids jumped with excitement.

"Are you coming, too?" Skylar asked me.

"I wish I could," I told her. "But I have an errand to run." I gave Sage a tight hug. "Do you have dinner plans?"

"We're eating with their parents tonight. Are you free tomorrow?" she said, still clinging to my neck.

For all our sisterly sniping, I was beyond glad that Sage was here. Especially with everything that was happening.

"All day," I said. "Unless I end up getting arrested."

Her green eyes darkened for a moment. "Don't even joke about it. I'll see you in the morning."

I exchanged fist bumps with the kids and stood near the edge of the walkway, waving until Sage, Skylar, and Dylan joined the line at the ice cream stand. As I walked back to my car I mused that if I *did* want to trail Antonio, I'd needed help from someone who drove like an absolute lunatic. As luck would have it, I knew just the perfect candidate for the job.

~ ~ ~ ~ ~ ~ ~ ~ ~ ~

I cornered Felix in the library off the foyer and shared my plan. He started out nodding along when I told him about Detective Drummond running down additional suspects, but when I reached the part where the two of us would park behind the tall cypress trees lining Antonio Santos' driveway, his eyes widened and he sort of shrank back against the wall. "You're joking, right?" he asked in a hopeful tone.

"No, I'm serious. Listen. I think Amber's affair was with Antonio. He showed up after the party. I saw him when I was leaving."

"What? Why didn't you tell me that earlier?"

I repeated the same explanation I'd given Detective Drummond and added, "I remember thinking he was meeting Alayna."

Felix roared with laughter. "Alayna? Yeah, I don't think so."

I cocked my head. Alayna was tall and lithe, with glossy black hair and warm brown eyes. She was serious and quiet, but I generally figured that was because she worked full-time for the Patricks and spent her evenings taking night classes at UCLA. She was probably tired.

"Why not? Because she's the *help?*" Maybe this apple wasn't as far from his rotten, old tree as I'd thought.

"Hey, no, it's not like that. She's just ... some kind of radical feminist man-hater."

"Alayna?"

He nodded, wide-eyed. "Trust me."

That didn't square with what little I knew about Alayna, but this entire conversation was a distraction from my mission.

"Whatever. Anyway, in light of what you said at lunch, I think Amber and Antonio may have been hot and heavy, which means he's an excellent candidate for her murder."

"So what?"

"So what? So maybe he's going to go out and dispose of evidence or ... something. We could catch him doing something incriminating. So go get your sporty little car and let's do this thing," I said in my peppiest voice.

"No offense, but I think you've seen too many movies."

I was gearing up to persuade him when the doorbell chimes rang, echoing through the eerily silent mansion. He swiveled his head toward the front door but made no movement to answer it. Through the French doors, I saw Alayna scurry through the hallway toward the door. She pulled open the door and engaged in a brief conversation with a man in a suit. I couldn't make out his face from the study, but I knew that voice: Detective Drummond was back. The man was like a bad rash.

"Come in. I'll go get Mr. Patrick," I heard her say.

She ushered the police officer inside and headed up the stairs to find Pat. Detective Drummond wiped his feet on the pristine white doormat (seriously, who uses a *white* doormat?) and clasped his hands together behind his back. He looked ill at ease and out of place in the vast, marble entryway. I knew exactly how he felt; I'd spent the first month or so of my employment tiptoeing around the house as if it were a museum.

I turned my attention back to Felix, but his eyes were still pinned on Detective Drummond, who stood shifting his weight from side to side just inside the door. Felix's hopeful expression gave me pause. He dashed past me and out into the hallway. I trailed behind him to see what he was up to.

"Detective," he called as he crossed the expansive space, "you have impeccable timing."

Detective Drummond turned toward Felix quickly, evidently startled by his loud, cheery greeting. "Mr. Patrick," he said stiffly. Then his eyes drifted over Felix's shoulder and locked on mine. He gave me a little smirk. "And, if it isn't Ms. Field. Aren't you supposed to be at the Santa Monica Pier with your sister?"

"I just came from there, actually. I wanted to talk to Fel—Mr. Patrick—about something." To my eternal aggravation, I felt my face grow warm and I knew I was blushing. And, of course, Detective Drummond would interpret that as some kind of confirmation of a romance between Felix and me. My next thought was to wonder why I cared what Detective Drummond believed, and *that* irritated me even further.

Meanwhile, both men were staring at me with twin looks of bemusement. So, like a complete loser, I chose that moment to trip over my own feet and go flying across the hallway. Just as I was thinking Alayna must have waxed the floors because I was picking up speed, a pair of strong hands caught me and stopped my fall. I looked up into my rescuer's face. Alayna's eyes met mine; I could see her trying to hold back her laughter.

"Uh, thanks," I managed as I righted myself. She'd come down the stairs at the exact right time.

"No problem," she said before turning to Detective Drummond. "Mr. Patrick is indisposed. Could you come back tomorrow around lunchtime? He's quite busy with ... making Mrs. Amber's arrangements."

Translation: he's working his way through a bottle of Hendrick's and is far too sloppy to be seen at the moment.

Detective Drummond's knitted brow and pursed lips indicated that he shared my skepticism. "He understands this is a murder investigation and every hour that passes makes it exponentially less likely that we'll find the killer? His failure to cooperate could mean his wife's murderer goes free."

Alayna was unmoved. "I'll give him the message, detective." She paused at the foot of the stairs, one hand on the railing, and glanced over her shoulder, letting her eyes rest on me. Then she said, "Although I don't see why you have to do any heavy lifting to find the person who made that gravy."

She started up the staircase and was gone before I caught her meaning.

"Hey," I sputtered uselessly. "That's not fair."

I wheeled around to face Detective Drummond, as my heart pounded in my chest. Did Alayna really think

I killed Amber? Did *everyone* think so? Visions of orange prison jumpsuits and blue-inked tats swam in my head.

The police officer gave me a sympathetic smile and said, "She's right, you know. Detective Sullivan is itching to charge you. She's given me one day to find her a better suspect. But if your boss isn't in the mood to answer questions, there's a limit to how much I can do."

My throat was a dry as the Mojave, and my legs swayed, threatening to give out. Felix reached over and grabbed my elbow to steady me.

He appealed to Detective Drummond. "This is crazy. Rosemary didn't kill my stepmother. Can I answer your questions instead of my dad?"

I focused on continuing to breathe. Detective Drummond shook his head. "We'll give it a shot, but they're fairly intimate in nature."

"Just ask him. He knew about Amber's affair. Maybe he can help," I urged.

"Right," Felix said eagerly. "Amber was sleeping with someone. Rosemary thinks it might be our neighbor. You should talk to—"

"I already did. Antonio Santos and Mrs. Patrick were not having an affair."

The bubble of hope that had begun to rise in my chest as Felix spoke popped instantly. "You talked to him? He denied it?" I asked.

"No. I didn't have to. Clay Carlson showed up at the station this afternoon, distraught and demanding to know what we were doing to find the person who killed his girlfriend."

Clay Carlson? Amber was screwing her costar? How ... cliche. I sneaked a glance at Felix out of the corner of my eye. His mouth was twisted into a wry grin.

"That sounds about right," he said. "Amber lacked imagination. An affair with her leading man would be right up her alley."

Another tiny hope bubble formed. "Okay, so maybe he killed her," I said with way too much enthusiasm.

Detective Buzzkill shook his head. "He's got an alibi. He was being interviewed live on the air on WKSTR's radio show about the new movie. He left the party with the film's publicist at eleven o'clock and the interview ran from twelve thirty to one."

"He did an interview in the middle of the night?" I said in disbelief.

"It happened. I listened to the recording," the police officer shrugged.

"Awfully convenient," I muttered.

"That's how alibis work, Rosemary. They conveniently make it impossible for the suspect to have committed the crime. Besides, the man was very clearly torn apart by her death."

"He's an actor," Felix observed.

"True, but he should win an Oscar for this performance if it was an act. Mr. Carlson seems to be unique among Amber's circle in that he actually liked the woman. He may even have loved her."

The notion that someone could genuinely love Amber Patrick was too weird for me to wrap my mind around. Judging from the pained look on Felix's face, he felt the same way.

Finally, Felix said, "I guess anything's possible. But, look around, detective. Do you see all the fruit baskets and arrangements of flowers that we *haven't* received? There are people quietly rejoicing all over town that the wicked witch is dead."

"So I've heard. But, as I explained to Ms. Field, that fact doesn't really help her."

"Well, maybe Amber was sleeping with Carlson *and* Santos. Maybe Santos found out," Felix ventured.

"Mr. Carlson showed us some text messages. It appears he and Mrs. Patrick were very serious about their relationship. She was planning to divorce your father so she could take her relationship with Mr. Carlson public. I don't think she was stepping out on him."

I couldn't speak. I tried to push back the wave of terror and panic that was washing over me. If Pat wasn't going to cooperate and give the cops some decent leads, I was going to end up in jail.

After a long moment, Detective Drummond cleared his throat. "I'm doing everything I can. I'm going to head over to the lab and light a fire under the forensic scientists—see if I can find out anything from the reports. Mr. Patrick, if you want to help Ms. Field, I suggest you talk to your father. If Amber was planning to leave him for Clay Carlson, he's a viable suspect. However, I'm not sure how you feel about implicating your father to save your *friend.*" He set his mouth in a grim line and let himself out.

I locked eyes with Felix. His eyes mirrored back the fear I felt.

"You don't think my dad killed her. Do you?"

I didn't know how to answer. Pat was the one who'd told me about the menu change. So he knew I'd be making gravy and had had all day to sneak some nuts into it. He also knew that his wife was cheating on him. And he *was* the one who found Amber's body. Means, motive, and opportunity. Check, check, check. Add in the fact that he had a mean streak and ... well, yeah, as a matter of fact, I did. But, could I really *say* that to Pat's son? Even if I was secretly hoping his dad was a murderer because that ugly fact would save my hide?

"Umm ..."

Pain etched itself across Felix's taut face. "Really?"

"I don't know," I said miserably. "Do you think it's completely impossible?"

"Of course!" he shot back instantly.

I was about to apologize, when his father came storming down the stairs.

"Is that blasted cop gone?" Pat demanded.

"Yes. He just left. Dad, he needs to talk to you." Felix's voice was hesitant but determined.

Pat wheeled around, red-faced. "I'm not talking to the cops, you moron. I have things to do," he said.

I shrank into the wall, trying to make myself invisible. Pat had a lot of ire. And if he needed a target, I imagined I'd make a handy one. I shouldn't have worried about that, though, because he glowered at his son for a moment longer and then stomped toward the back of the house. A moment later the door leading from the house to the garage slammed shut. The engine of Pat's Mercedes roared to life.

Felix grabbed my hand and started pulling me along the hallway. "Come on!" he urged.

"Where are we going?" I asked as I jogged to keep up with him.

"You wanted to play private investigator, didn't you? We're going to follow my dad."

"Then what?"

"I'm going to make him talk to me. The cops are going in the wrong direction—you didn't kill Amber, but neither did he. We have to get this straightened out."

Eight

I WAS STILL TRYING TO buckle my seatbelt when Felix peeled out of the garage. As the Boxster raced down the curvy driveway leading to the canyon road, I gripped the handle of the passenger door and offered up a silent prayer. *This was your brilliant idea,* I chided myself.

Against my better judgment, I peeked at the speedometer. "I don't think it's going to be helpful if we get pulled over for speeding," I ventured mildly.

Felix glanced over at me. "Where's your sense of adventure, Rosemary?" He flashed me a grin and zoomed toward the electronic gates that fronted his family's property.

For a moment I thought we were going to crash into them as they began their oh-so-gradual opening. But he eased off the gas until the gap was just large enough for his sports car to zip through. As he careened out of the driveway and onto the road, I pushed myself back against the seat and closed my eyes.

After a few moments, I felt the car begin to slow. I opened my eyes and resumed breathing. "Did you decide to take pity on me?"

"Ha, you wish. I just don't want Dad to know we're back here. Going to let him get a little further ahead." Felix nodded toward the windshield.

I peered out through the glass and saw taillights winding down the road ahead of us.

"Don't let him get so far ahead of you that you lose him."

"You sure are demanding." Felix shook his head at me in frustration. "There's only one way down out of the canyon. We can give him a little room."

We lapsed into silence. I figured the less I distracted him while he navigated the hairpin turns, the better. In the meantime, for the first time since the police had pounded on my door hours earlier, I thought through everything I knew about Amber's death. And the more I thought, the less sense it made.

When the mountain flattened out and we reached the wide city streets, I decided it was safe to talk. "How much do you know about Amber's nut allergy?" I asked.

He allowed two cars to merge between us and his father's vehicle but kept his eyes trained on the Mercedes, while he answered. "Enough to know she was deathly allergic. She was worried enough that she had her doctor come to the house and show me and my dad how to use the Epi-pen. Why?"

"If she'd eaten gravy—or anything—with nuts in it during the party, wouldn't she have had an immediate reaction? The police said it was around one in the morning when she went into anaphylaxis. The party ended before midnight."

"I think she would have had trouble breathing immediately, yeah. Maybe she got herself a midnight snack after everyone left?"

I shook my head. "Come on, you know Amber didn't *snack.* And, even if she had gone looking for something to eat, I took all the leftovers. So she couldn't have eaten food from the party."

"You took them?" His tone of voice held the barest hint of employer/employee admonishment.

"I donated them to a homeless shelter. Amber knew that's what I did with all the leftovers when she entertained."

"Oh. Good idea."

He slowed the car as, up ahead, his father braked for a red light. I was itching to call Detective Drummond and tell him to ask the forensic investigators or the coroner—somebody—about whether there was such a thing as a delayed allergic reaction. Maybe they'd stop trying to pin the murder on me. I also made a mental note to tell him to find out if Loving Hands had any of the gravy left. I doubted they would; Deb made it a point to use every scrap of food that came her way. But if she hadn't, they could test the gravy and see that it didn't contain nuts. My heart started to pound with excitement, and I was pulling out my phone to call and ask her myself, when Felix slammed on the breaks and I pitched forward.

"Hey!" I protested.

"Sorry." He jerked the wheel to the right, and we zipped down a side street.

"What are you doing? Your dad didn't turn off." I dropped the phone back into my bag and turned to glare at him.

"Settle down. I know where he's going. We're going to take a shortcut so we can get in position and watch him when he arrives," he told me in a self-satisfied voice.

"Oh. So, tell me, Sherlock. What's his destination?"

"You should know. Recognize this neighborhood?"

I stared out the passenger window. Large stucco apartment buildings, boxy and close together, flashed by. I squinted into the dark and tried to make out something that looked familiar, but I couldn't. I'm sort of spatially challenged. As in, whenever I visit Thyme in New York, she threatens to pin an index card to my shirt with her contact information on it in case I wander off and can't make my way back to her apartment. As in, once, when Sage was living in D.C., I left her apartment near Chinatown to meet a friend in Georgetown for lunch. Instead of taking the Metro, I drove and somehow managed to travel from Point A to Point B—located about two and a half miles apart in the city's northwest quadrant—via both Maryland *and* Virginia. So, no, I didn't have the slightest clue where we were.

"I give up," I said.

He eased the car into a parking spot and killed the engine. I grabbed my purse and met him on the sidewalk. He draped an arm around my shoulder, and I shivered as a crackle of electricity made its way up my spine. I told myself the chill was due to the cool night air and not the heat from his skin. He turned me about forty-five degrees to the right and pointed down a narrow alleyway.

"See that brick wall with the gate set into it?"

I looked in the direction he was pointing. "Yes."

"Behind that gate is the garden where we ate lunch today."

~ ~ ~ ~ ~ ~ ~ ~ ~ ~

My heart was pounding so loudly as we crept along the narrow alley that I kept waiting for Felix to tell me to keep it down. Leaving the car and sneaking into the garden to spy on Pat seemed like a medium-bad idea to me, but he was dead set on it. So here we were, tiptoeing through the trashcans.

"Are you sure your dad won't drive past your car?" I whispered.

He turned and gave me an exasperated look over his shoulder. "I'm sure. That was the whole point of parking where we did. He'll come up from Santa Monica Boulevard and go into the apartment building from the front."

I trotted along behind him. I won't lie. My apprehension about confronting Pat was mixed with anticipation and a little bit of heady excitement. I felt like we were doing something thrilling, if possibly dangerous. Felix must have been feeling the same way because he glanced back again and grinned at me.

"Come on," he urged, grabbing my hand to pull me even with him.

We came to a stop in front of the wrought iron gate and stood staring at the dark apartment. No lights shined through the windows. No shadows moved inside. The place was dark and quiet. The only illumination came from a security light mounted on the trellis that sheltered the patio. Felix took his keys from his pocket and eased a long silver key into the gate's lock. He turned it, and the gate swung silently toward us. He stopped its motion with one hand and gently nudged me through the opening.

"It looks like we beat him here. We'll go in through the garden. Follow my lead," he whispered in my ear after pulling the gate shut and locking it behind him.

His warm breath tickled my hair. He reached for my hand again and laced his fingers through mine. If you'd have told me yesterday that I'd be sneaking around holding hands with Felix Patrick, I'd have told you you were a lunatic. But here we were. Just us, the stars fighting through the cloud cover overhead, and a pale crescent moon. The garden was as lush and fragrant in the night as it had been midday. The sole difference was that the blooms were closed up as if they were sleeping. The only sounds were the tinkle of the water feature and the soft crunch of crushed stones underfoot as we wended our way along the path.

He stopped suddenly as we reached the fountain, and I stumbled into him.

"Sorry. What's wrong?" I asked, any illusions that we were taking a romantic walk shattered by the way he tensed his shoulders and held up his palm.

"Hear that?"

I strained to listen. A car's engine was drawing nearer. As the low growl grew louder, he stiffened even further.

"That's him," he said.

I had my doubts as to whether a person could really identify a specific Mercedes' engine by its sound. But his voice was full of conviction, so I decided to take his comment at face value. As the car pulled into the driveway that led from the front of the house, Felix squeezed my hand so tightly my knuckles ached. I squeezed back.

"Now what?" I whispered, as the engine turned off and the sound of a car door slamming shut echoed through the courtyard.

He pulled me to the side of the path and led me through the dense magnolias to a side porch I hadn't even noticed during our interrupted lunch. The porch abutted the kitchen, judging by the gleaming appliances visible through the French doors. He hurried to the edge of the porch and shimmied between the side of the house and the fence that separated the building from the stucco home next door.

I followed suit and we side-stepped along the fence until we reached a large window that looked directly into a small parlor off the kitchen. The window was framed by cream-colored linen curtains that were tied back and afforded us a perfect view. A small Tiffany-style lamp cast a dim light in the room. I could make out a fireplace with an ornate mantle and two Queen Anne chairs. They were covered in a muted silk stripe. Between the chairs, a small glass and metal bar held two rows of glasses and several decanters filled with various liquors.

Suddenly light flooded the interior of the house. More out of reflex than anything else, I drew back from the window and pressed myself against the edge of the building. I noticed Felix did the same on the opposite side of the window. I held my breath and listened to Pat bang around in the house. He must have passed through the parlor and gone into the kitchen because the back of the apartment was flooded with light and the door to the patio banged open.

I sought Felix's eyes frantically. *Was Pat coming out back?*

Felix mouthed 'it's okay' and gave me a reassuring smile. Sure enough, after an excruciatingly long minute, the door banged shut and the outdoor lights went off. I exhaled and peeked through the window. Pat was standing near the bar with a handful of freshly picked mint and a white marble mortar and pestle.

Ah, he was just muddling mint for a drink. I exhaled and nearly went limp with relief. I considered that perhaps I wasn't cut out for this secret spy stuff and flashed Felix an embarrassed grin. He looked as though he were about to say something but the sudden roar of a car engine cut off the words before he formed them.

I'm no gearhead, but even I could tell this car was much noisier and more muscular than the Mercedes had been. Instead of purring, it roared. It sounded as loud as a racecar as it pulled into the driveway behind Pat's car. I felt my eyes go wide. Felix motioned for me to join him on his side of the window. I crouched low, under the window, just in case, and duck walked over to him.

We peered through the window as Pat hurried toward the front of the house with a glass in each hand. I sort of figured Pat was meeting his mistress, but I nearly fell over when I saw who came striding into view and grabbed Pat in a long, tight embrace.

"Is that ... Antonio Santos?" Felix asked.

I blinked. When I opened my eyes, the scene hadn't changed. "Yep."

We watched as Pat pulled back, held the racecar driver at arm's length, and drank in the sight of him. Pat's entire face softened from hard-edged music mogul to adoring partner.

"I didn't know your dad was gay," I said stupidly.

Felix was speechless. I guess he didn't either.

I'm not sure what he would have done next if sirens hadn't pierced the air from all directions. A black and white patrol car screeched to a halt out front, most likely blocking the driveway unless television shows had lied to me. A second unit rolled through the alley and parked just in front of the gate. Two figures emerged from the car and cleared the low gate like hurdlers in a track and field event. One headed directly for the back door, gun drawn. The other made a beeline straight toward the side of the house where we were hiding.

Felix pressed his finger against his lips as if maybe I'd been planning to blurt out a greeting.

Bright light arced over us. I shielded my eyes and turned to squint into the face of none other than Detective Drummond. He trained the flashlight on us much longer and more directly than I personally thought was strictly necessary.

"I wish I could say this is a surprise," he cracked.

Beside me, Felix was covering his face. "Would you turn that thing off already?" he demanded.

Detective Drummond took his time lowering the beam so it pointed at the ground. Then he jabbed a finger at us in the air. "Don't go anywhere. After we take your father into custody, we're going to want to talk to you," he said to Felix. Then he turned to me. "Same goes for you, Ms. Field." I figured it had to be my imagination, but I thought I heard a note of disappointment in his voice—as if he expected better from me.

"You're ... arresting my dad?" Felix sputtered.

He suddenly looked even younger than he was, like a lost little boy, really. It made my heart ache.

Detective Drummond apparently was deficient in the sympathy category because he didn't try to soften his response. "It looks like Mr. Patrick has a pretty compelling motive for murder. Mr. Carlson reached out to Detective Sullivan a few hours ago with some information that he'd held back from his original interview because he didn't want us to get the wrong idea about Mrs. Patrick. After giving it some thought, he reconsidered. It's a good thing because his information is going to nail Roland Patrick's hide to the wall."

"What's this mystery information?" I asked as I reached for Felix's hand. Don't get me wrong, I was ecstatic to know that I wasn't going to be charged, but I also know firsthand what it feels like to learn that a parent has feet of clay. I squeezed his hand tightly.

Detective Drummond raised an eyebrow at the gesture but continued. "In her divorce preparations, Mrs. Patrick hired an attorney, a forensic accountant, and a private investigator to see if she could come up any grounds to nullify the prenuptial agreement that Mr. Patrick made her sign. The private investigator found out about Mr. Patrick's homosexual affair with Mr. Santos. Mrs. Patrick apparently decided to blackmail her husband with the evidence of his relationship and force him to agree to spousal support notwithstanding the existence of the prenup."

I felt sick. Amber really had been a horrible wench.

I sneaked a look at Felix and tried to guess what he was feeling, but his face was set in stone. "That's still not proof he killed her."

"No, it's not," Detective Drummond agreed. "But the forensic reports came back."

"And?" I interjected. I couldn't help it.

"There was no evidence of cashews present in Amber's stomach contents," he said. He waited for that to sink in. "But the lab geeks did find peanut oil."

"Peanut oil?" I repeated. "I don't keep peanut oil in the kitchen. I couldn't use it in any recipes. And Amber would have freaked out if she'd found in her house."

The police officer nodded. "Right. We didn't find any peanut oil in the kitchen. But testing showed the oil had been added to a partially consumed bottle of 2007 merlot found near Mrs. Patrick's body in her dressing room."

The image of Amber tottering up the stairs with her hand wrapped around an open bottle of red wine flashed in my mind.

"Someone put it in her wine?" Felix asked.

"Yes, and in light of the new information, we like your father for it."

Felix shook his head in disbelief. "I want to talk to him."

Detective Drummond twisted his lips into a knot as he considered his response.

"Hang on. How'd you know they were here—Pat and Santos?"

He turned to me with an unreadable expression. "We didn't. In light of Mr. Carlson's new information, Detective Sullivan authorized me to do what you had wanted all along. I've been following Santos. When we arrived and saw Mr. Patrick's Mercedes in the driveway, my partner called for backup. Good thing we're virtually around the corner from the station."

"Oh," I managed.

He turned back to Felix. "Once Detective Sullivan radios me that he's in custody, I'll give you five minutes."

He didn't wait for thanks or a response of any kind. He just turned on his heel and jogged over to the uniformed officer waiting for him by the kitchen door.

I swallowed hard and waited for Felix to say something. He didn't speak at first. I watched as he clenched and unclenched the muscles in his jaw, making his cheek tighten and relax, tighten and relax. My stomach was jumpy and unsettled as I tried to think of something appropriately supportive and understanding to say to a guy who just found out his father was about to be arrested for murdering his stepmother so his affair with another man wouldn't be uncovered. I suspected Hallmark probably had a card for this occasion, but I was coming up empty.

"Um ..." I began, ever eloquent.

"I can't believe it," he whispered, more to himself than to me.

"Felix—"

He continued, "I mean, the affair with Santos. I can believe that. Now that I think about it, it fits. He never brought any girlfriends home when I was growing up. He never talked about women."

"Then why would he marry Amber?" My curiosity overcame my social ineptitude.

He shrugged. "For the publicity, if I had to guess. The label hadn't had a big hit in a while. Sales were slumping. But their marriage was huge news. Everything spiked after that." He said it as if it were a no-brainer: Record sales down? Marry a movie star.

"Then what's so hard to believe?"

"That he'd allow her to blackmail him—or that he'd resort to killing her. That's not dad's style. He doesn't shy away from a fight."

I hated to be the one to point it out, but I figured it would be better coming from me than from Detective She-Devil Sullivan. "Unless he was trying to protect you," I suggested in a soft voice.

His head snapped back and he searched my eyes with his. "Me? What do you mean?"

I cleared my throat. "Like you said, your dad isn't exactly a shrinking violet. But he lived a closeted life for who knows how long? The most reasonable explanation is that he wasn't sure how his sexuality would affect you. And if the protective shell he'd worked so hard to create was threatened ... I don't know, Felix. I don't have kids. But I understand the instinct to protect them can be overwhelming."

My eyes actually filled with tears as I thought of Felix's father denying his own sexuality to protect his son and, inevitably, contrasted that behavior with my own parents, who turned their backs on their three daughters and left us to clean up their expensive mess. *Get a grip, Rosemary. Felix needs a friend right now. You can blubber about your bad luck later.*

His lower lip trembled. "Do you really think that he could have killed her—to protect *me*?"

"Maybe?" I ventured.

At that moment, the uniformed officer who'd accompanied Detective Drummond poked his head out the back door and swiveled his head toward us. "Sir, Detective Drummond said you can have five minutes with the suspect. Understand that I will remain in the room and he will be restrained in handcuffs."

Felix's entire body sagged. "Thank you, officer. But I've changed my mind. I don't need to speak to him."

The police officer cocked his head. For a moment, I thought he was going to try to convince Felix to talk to his dad but then he nodded. "That's your call." And then he was gone.

That left me to do the convincing. "Wait a second. I didn't say your dad *did* kill Amber. Just that you should consider the possibility. Don't turn your back on him. You should talk to him, Felix."

"I just ... can't. Not yet." His eyes met mine with a pleading look, and I remembered he was barely into his twenties.

I opened my arms to hug him, and he stepped close to me. I could feel his heart racing through his thin shirt. I rubbed his back in a constant, circular motion until the rhythm of his heart slowed to something less frantic than a hummingbird's.

Nine

I SLINKED INTO THE KITCHEN in a pair of boxers and an oversized UCLA tee shirt, both borrowed from Felix. The quiet, spotless space with its gleaming appliances and wide expanse of counters looked completely different in the pre-dawn light, approached from the rear stairs as a well-rested overnight guest rather than through the employees' entrance as a harried, if highly paid, worker bee.

I was standing on tiptoes on the cold terrazzo reveling in the feeling when a voice drawled, "So how do you take your coffee?"

Felix. I immediately crossed my arms in front of my chest in embarrassment and wished I'd taken the time to get dressed. "Uh, just some hemp milk, please. And thank you." Another new sensation—Felix waiting on *me* in this kitchen.

He quirked his lips into a smile and crossed the kitchen to the refrigerator. "You're out of luck. I tossed all of Amber's stupid food yesterday afternoon."

I tried not to react visibly to the casual meanness of his action. "Oh?"

"Yep. The cops took everything they considered evidence. What was left went into the garbage." He leaned into the fridge and reemerged holding a glass container. "Full fat cow's milk. Want some?"

"Uh, sure. Just a splash."

He handed me a glazed mug filled with coffee and then leaned closer than was absolutely necessary to pour in the milk. Rows of goosebumps rose on my arms in reaction when he brushed my shoulder.

"Are you cold?" He gave me a look that took in my bare legs and the thin tee shirt.

"No."

"That shirt looks good on you. You should keep it," he remarked, letting his gaze linger.

I considered and rejected several responses. I took a long swallow of coffee and shifted my weight from side to side. Finally, I said, "About last night ..."

"Thank you for staying," he said, lowering his eyes so that his long, thick eyelashes seemed to brush against his cheeks.

A wave of warmth rushed over me, washing away my snarky, embarrassed discomfort at standing, barely dressed, in the kitchen with a man who somehow managed to look delectable when he rolled out of bed.

"You don't have to thank me."

I nearly spilled my coffee in surprise when he grabbed me and wrapped me in a tight hug. After a moment, he pulled back and kissed me on the forehead, letting his lips brush gently over my brow.

It was a tender moment. Or, at least it would have been, if Alayna hadn't chosen that precise time to burst into the room, banging and clattering cleaning supplies in her wake.

We both jumped.

She stared at us. "Oh, sorry," she said in a tone that was anything but.

I would never have said Alayna and I were besties, but we were friendly. We got along pretty well and had always looked out for one another when Amber was rampaging. But the way she curled her lip me made me think I had badly misjudged our relationship. Then it dawned on me that my behavior, not to mention my attire, probably seemed wildly inappropriate.

I smoothed down my hair. "It's not how it looks," I told her. I flashed Felix a desperate glancing, hoping he'd chime in in agreement, but he just leaned back against the counter and drank his coffee. He wasn't smiling, but his eyes crinkled in amusement.

He clearly wasn't going to be any help.

I turned back to Alayna.

She shot me a blank look and said, "It's none of my business. Are you working today?"

I hadn't thought it was possible to feel more intensely uncomfortable than I already did, but her question ramped up my discomfort to eleven on a scale of one to ten. Her question reminded me that I was Felix's father's employee—a small fact that made my appearance in the kitchen at no o'clock in the morning tangled in an embrace with Felix while wearing his tee shirt and boxer shorts (which she no doubt knew, considering she did the laundry) seem like something out of a soap opera. Or, even worse, one of Amber's movies.

"Um, no," I mumbled, unable to meet her eye or stop myself from blushing. "In fact, I need to go. I'm meeting my sister."

I rushed past her and ran up the back stairs two at a time. I threw on my wrinkled clothes from the day before and gathered my hair into a low, messy ponytail. I grabbed my shoes and purse and flew back down the stairs. I was out the door and starting my car before Felix or Alayna had a chance to say another word.

~ ~ ~ ~ ~ ~ ~ ~ ~ ~

Sage, however, had lots of words to say. Once she was finished gaping at me fish-like, that is.

"You ... you slept with him?" she whispered, leaning across the table.

I nearly sprayed my mimosa all over the tablecloth. "What? No, I slept *over*. He didn't want to be alone," I choked out the words in a hurry.

"Oh." She sipped her drink and considered my answer. "Are you sure?"

"Yes, I'm sure. I think I'd notice. I hope I would, at least."

She laughed at that. Sage's laugh is infectious— sunny and real. Before I knew it, I was laughing, too. Sitting there in the fancy pants restaurant she'd chosen for brunch, with fresh-cut flowers, crisp white linens, and delicious mimosas, I felt like my carefree former self, the Rosemary who existed before crushing debt, a soul-sucking job, and suspicion of murder clouded her days.

Her laugh died down gradually. Her eyes sparkled conspiratorially and she said, "Well, good for you for not taking advantage of him during his time of emotional need."

If she only knew.

After we'd left the scene of his father's arrest, I figured he'd drop me at my car and then go lick his wounds in private. That's what I'd have done. Instead, when we reached my car, he hadn't killed the engine. He'd put the car into park and turned to me with what can only be described as a beseeching look. "Rosemary, stay with me. Please."

Five simple words. Two very short sentences. But there'd been no resisting his desperation; he was like a lost little boy. So I'd agreed to stay subject to certain ground rules: I was there to provide moral support and company only. I would sleep in the guest bedroom next door to his room. He'd agreed readily to my stipulations. But I had a suspicion that if I hadn't laid out the rules, we'd have had a very different night.

"Hello? Did I lose you?"

"Huh?" I looked up. Sage was waving her hand in front of my face. "Sorry."

"Don't be. But snap out of it. This is probably my only free window of time before we go back East. Let's take advantage of the fact that Chip and Muffy want to present the picture of the All-American family at the press event."

"Having a nanny is un-American?"

"Attachment parenting consultant," she said, correcting me out of habit.

"Even better."

She arched an eyebrow. "Apparently, their media consultant thinks my presence would alienate Chip's base."

"He has a base to alienate? Is he a golfer or a politician?"

"Whatever. It's a day off for me." She waved away the topic. "Let's talk about you."

"Me? I don't have anything interesting going on."

The waiter materialized with blueberry ricotta pancakes for me and house-made yogurt and granola for Sage. Sage, apparently having not picked up any Southern manners during her time in South Carolina, didn't bother to wait until he finished refilling our water glasses to call me out.

"Right. Nothing interesting in your life. Accused of murdering your movie star boss, canoodling with her smoking hot son, and flirting with the police officer assigned to investigate the case. Just another ho-hum weekend in the life of a holistic chef, huh?"

Her sparkling laughter only intensified when the eavesdropping waiter got so wrapped up in her recitation that he let the ice water flow over the edge of the glass and pool into a good-sized puddle on the table.

"I think it's full," I told him, pointing to Sage's glass.

"Oh! Oh, geez. I'm sorry. I wasn't paying attention," he said as he mopped up the water with a white cloth. Then, as devoid of shame as any aspiring actor ought to be, he stared right at me. "You worked for Amber Patrick? Is it true her husband did it?" he breathed.

I fixed Sage with a dirty look before answering him. "Mr. Patrick's in custody. I don't know what, if anything, the police have charged him with," I said diplomatically. The *Los Angeles Times* had run a short article, barely more than a barebones blurb, that morning. Detective Sullivan had been tight-lipped, and the article had been short on details, including the fact of the Patricks' respective extramarital activities. I figured the entertainment media would dig those up soon enough.

The waiter turned and sauntered away, a little deflated by the lack of juicy details. I continued to shoot daggers at Sage.

"Sorry," she mumbled into her champagne flute.

"Forget it. What did you mean though, about flirting with a police officer? Are you talking about me and Detective Drummond?"

"No, Rosie, you and Detective Sullivan," she deadpanned.

"I'm serious. I wasn't ... I didn't ... I'm not flirting with that cop," I finally managed to stammer.

"Oh, come on."

"I'm not," I insisted. I dug into my pancakes. "But I'm curious why you think I am."

"For one thing, he's supposed to be a professional hardass. You'd expect him to keep his distance from a ... um, suspect. But he didn't. He came mooning around to try to help you."

"Maybe that's because he knew I was innocent, Sage."

She shrugged and swirled her yogurt around with her spoon. "Maybe. I just thought I picked up on a vibe.

Anyway, I notice you aren't protesting the canoodling with Felix part."

"Mainly because I don't know what canoodling means," I told her. I leaned back and drank in the wonderful normalcy of sitting in a nice restaurant, catching up with my sister over a meal someone else prepared, and let a wave of yearning for my old life wash over me.

"Me neither," Sage admitted with a laugh. "But it's what Mom always used to say when you were making out with Thor Martin down on the dock instead of practicing your violin like you were supposed to be. So I figured it fit."

"Oh, Thor. That poor guy. I wonder if the other podiatrists make fun of his name." You know your parents screwed up when *I* think your name was ill advised.

"Doubt it. Mom said he goes by T. Charles now."

I narrowed my eyes. Sage was the quintessential middle child, focused on personal relationships and connections. You know that friend you have who knows everyone and is always putting together Friend A, who needs to buy a house, with Friend B, who just happens to be selling one? And if they find they need a realtor or lawyer or building inspector, no worries, she's friends with one? Yeah, that's Sage. In addition to her network of friends, she maintains our family ties, too. She sends birthday cards to the most distant relatives and attends any and all family reunions. And now she'd mentioned our mom twice in the space of a minute.

"When was the last time you talked to Mom?" I asked with all the subtlety of Detective Sullivan.

She immediately dropped her eyes and stared at the tablecloth. "Last April. Same as you and Thyme."

I just finished my drink and waited. Sage has always been a terrible liar; she can't even manage a decent lie of omission. And after approximately twelve seconds of silence, she cracked. "She does email me every once in a while."

"You're in email contact with Mom?" I said, wanting to be absolutely sure I'd heard her correctly.

"I wouldn't call it being in contact. Maybe once every other month, she sends me a very short email to let me know that she and dad are okay and to ask about all of us. That's it," she said in a hurry.

"Tell me you've handed these over to the cops, at least." I still really couldn't believe what I was hearing.

"Well, no," she admitted. "But I don't think they'd be useful to the authorities, Rosemary. She doesn't say anything about where they are. And I think she's using burner email addresses."

I cocked my head in disbelief. Our mother, who just months earlier was possibly the last person in North America to maintain an AOL account and use a dial-up connection, was now suddenly floating around some-where in international waters, accessing the Internet and creating disposable email addresses? "Really?"

"Really. Thyme thinks ..." she trailed off and finished her mimosa in one large gulp, looking slightly green as she realized what she'd done.

"Oh, Thyme knows about this? Has Mom been emailing her, too?" I couldn't manage to keep the hurt out of my voice.

"No, just me, Rosie. I swear." She reached across the table and grabbed my hand. "I told Thyme about the emails to see if she could figure out how to find them, and she said it looks like Mom's masking her location through a series of proxy addresses."

I laughed in complete disbelief. "Okay, sure. So, I'm just curious—why did you and Thyme decide to keep these innocuous, untraceable communications a big secret, hmm?"

She cleared her throat and took her time forming an answer. "Mainly because we knew it would make you mad. Madder, I mean. You know, Rosemary, you're *really* angry with her and Dad."

"Wait. *You're* not?"

"Of course I am. Thyme is, too. But not like you. I think we both can understand that they did a really crappy thing, but that they were probably in over their heads and panicked."

I couldn't believe what I was hearing. "They *panicked?* They're adults. Adults who racked up a half-million dollars in debt and waltzed away, making it our problem."

She was chewing on her lower lip. "Well, to be fair, we made it our problem. We could have refused to take over the resort and let the creditors have it. We *chose* to try to save it."

"Do you regret that now?"

"No, of course not. We agreed we didn't want to see the place paved over. It holds too many memories to let it go without a fight. Not to mention, I really think that we can turn it around and make it profitable once we dig ourselves out from the hole we're in."

I exhaled in relief. "Then what are you trying to say?"

"We have to own our decision. And using our energy sending negative vibes into the universe directed at Mom and Dad isn't really helpful."

I sighed and pushed my plate away, suddenly not hungry. "You think I'm judgmental. Is that what all that hippy-dippy lingo is getting at?"

"You have a finely developed sense of right and wrong," she answered, the consummate diplomat.

Something about the phrasing made me laugh. When I caught my breath, I smiled across the table. "Okay, Sage. I don't want to fight with you. We don't get to spend much time together. Let's not waste it picking open old scabs."

She smiled back. "So ... Felix. Are you two a thing?"

"I don't know. We may be heading that way." I shrugged but my stomach flip-flopped with excitement at the prospect.

"He's really hot," she squealed.

I nodded. He really was.

"But ..." she hesitated and swirled yogurt around with her spoon, "his family life is a little screwed up. Are you sure he's stable?"

I almost snorted and dismissed the question with a jab about our own family, but something about the concern in her voice stopped me. I thought for a long moment about his angry outburst toward Amber and the way he turned his back on his father when the police showed up. "Not really. He's pretty young—and spoiled. And he's had a couple of pretty nasty shocks in the past couple days. He's probably a little emotional. But, at his core, he's a decent guy."

"Do you really believe that?"

I nodded. He had a pretty short fuse—especially where Amber was concerned—and it did have some irritating rich boy habits. But the fact remained he came to get me from the police station. He showed up when it counted. "Yeah, I do," I assured her.

"And you don't think it's kind of icky that he's been hitting on his family's employee?" she probed.

I sighed. "It's not like my job has a human resources department and all sorts of sexual harassment policies or anything. I'm sure he thinks his flirting is harmless.

And if it had really bothered me, I'd have said something. He'd have respected that. I know he would have."

"In that case, you might as well have some fun. You've earned it." She checked her watch and dabbed her mouth with the linen napkin. "I should get back and start packing up the kids' stuff for the flight back home." Then she locked eyes with me. "Unless you need me to stay until this Amber thing gets wrapped up. I will, you know. Muffy will understand."

"Nah," I said, putting down my credit card to pick up the check. "Everything's under control. I don't expect I'll have any more visits from your good friend Detective Dave."

Famous last words.

Ten

FTER A ROUND OF TEARFUL goodbye hugs, I dropped Sage off at the Wilshire Hotel and made my way through the cross-town traffic to my apartment. I squeezed into my assigned parking spot between two hulking SUVs and crossed the lot. I was lost in thought, obsessing over whether I was being too hard on my deadbeat parents, when someone whistled. It wasn't a 'hey sexy mama' whistle so much as a 'yo, cabbie' call. Loud, shrill, and all business.

I started and swiveled my head in the direction of the sound. Some white guy was leaning over the fence that separated my depressing, uninspired building from the depressing, uninspired building next door. I tossed him a quizzical, slightly annoyed look and was about to make a smart remark when I realized the whistler wasn't just a random guy. It was Detective Drummond. He looked so normal in street clothes that it took me a few seconds to place him.

"Oh, Detective Drummond. I didn't recognize you," I said as I walked over to the fence.

He leaned over the fence, laughing, and I was struck by the warmth in his brown eyes—like melted chocolate or hot cocoa or ... *Wait, what? Where did that come from?* I gave myself a little mental shake and tried to focus on what he was saying.

"I'm off duty. Call me Dave."

"Okay, Dave. Do you usually spend your free time skulking around in alleys?"

"No. Why? Are trying to see if we have hobbies in common?"

I wrinkled my brow in confusion and then remembered the way he'd found me and Felix the night before.

"Oh, ha. Uh, no." I smiled a little sheepishly.

"Hmm." His smile faded and his eyes got all intense and serious. "You need to be careful."

I stared at him blankly. "Oh-kay."

"I'm serious, Rosemary. Watch yourself around Felix." His gaze was intense.

I blinked. "Why?"

He coughed. "I'm not convinced his dad's good for Amber's murder."

I stared at him and tried to tease out the subtext that I was obviously missing. "Wait? Now you don't think Pat killed her? You think it was *Felix*?"

"I didn't say that. Maybe. I don't know. Sullivan's satisfied that it was Roland Patrick. The district attorney's satisfied. He's going to charge him in the morning."

"But?"

"But Antonio Santos swears up and down that Roland Patrick isn't a killer."

"That's it? He's in love, Detective ... Dave. Of course he can't admit his lover murdered his wife. For what it's worth, Felix thinks he did it."

"Does he? Or is he just content to have his dad take the fall for it?"

"Take the fall? Are you seriously suggesting it was Felix?" My irritation came out of nowhere. Some reasonable part of me realized I was already teed off about Sage and my mom's email correspondence, but that didn't stop me from taking it out on the handiest target.

"Whoa, whoa, whoa. I'm suggesting you might be getting mixed up in a family feud that doesn't involve you but sure could hurt you. That's all. I'm saying be careful—as a friend."

He spoke in the very measured, careful tone people used with volatile nut jobs. It did nothing to calm me down. In fact, it had the exact opposite effect.

"I can take care of myself, Detective Drummond," I said, putting heavy emphasis on his title to let him know we weren't friends. "Besides, I'm not getting mixed up with Felix. I told you before—we're not involved."

"Yeah, you said that. But that was before your sleepover," he said with a great big 'gotcha' smirk.

I stiffened. "Seems to me I should be more worried about the fact that I'm apparently being stalked by a member of law enforcement. Stop following me and leave me alone, Detective Drummond. Maybe instead of creeping around like a pervert you should pick a suspect and stick with it—you don't seem to be very good at the detecting thing."

He drew back like I'd physically assaulted him. His face turned a mottled red color, and, for a moment, I worried that I'd gone too far. But he got his anger under control impressively quickly and responded softly. "Fine. Have it your way. I've tried to warn you; my conscience is clear."

He turned from the fence without a backward glance. I could hear him whistling some old show tune as he strolled away.

I stomped off toward my apartment muttering under my breath.

~ ~ ~ ~ ~ ~ ~ ~ ~ ~

I peeled off my dry-clean only sundress and hung it back in the closet before it wrinkled, kicked off the cute sandals, and returned to my regularly scheduled program of slouchy tees and gym shorts. Despite the wardrobe upgrade, I was still spoiling for a fight when someone leaned on the buzzer for my unit. I could just picture Detective Drummond outside the building with his knowing smile.

I jabbed the intercom button. "Now what?"

"Uh, delivery for Ms. Field?" a tentative male voice, definitely not Detective Drummond's, responded.

"Oh. Sorry! Come on up." I buzzed him in.

I was still trying to remember what I could have ordered online in the past few days when the delivery guy rapped on my apartment door. I pulled it open. And instead of my usual brown-uniformed UPS guy bearing a Prime box, there was a black-suited stranger bearing a vase of colorful tulips. I stared at him.

"Rosemary Field?" he asked with a smile, thrusting the flowers toward me.

"Yes?" I answered uncertainly. "Are you sure you have the right Rosemary Field?"

He nodded and gestured toward the tiny envelope stuck into the middle of the flowers. I plucked it out and read the enclosed card:

> *Rosemary,*
> *How about a proper date?*
> *Jeeves will drive you to meet me.*
> *Fondly,*
> *Felix*

Fondly? What twenty-two-year-old guy sends his driver with flowers and signs a card '*fondly*'? I desperately wished Sage weren't jetting back to South Carolina at this precise moment. I could use a sisterly reality check. Catching Thyme up on everything that was going on would take far too long.

The driver gave me a concerned look. "Are you feeling okay?"

"What? Oh, yeah. I'm just surprised. Let me put these down and change. Just give me a minute."

"Take your time, ma'am. I'm at your disposal."

I narrowed my eyes and looked at him closely. "Is your name really Jeeves?"

"Nah, it's Marvin—Marvin Beany Shooks." He extended his right hand. "Jeeves is Felix's idea of a joke, I guess."

"Where did you come from, Marvin? I happen to know the Patricks don't have a personal driver," I pressed him as we shook hands. Come to think of it, I wondered why they didn't. They had a personal everything else—chef, maid, gardener, stylist, shopping consultant, you name it.

He nodded. "I'm employed by the record label. But when I'm not driving around vocalists and musicians, I'm at Pat's disposal. And, now, apparently Felix's."

His voice was devoid of judgment or emotion, but something about his word choice made me think Marvin wasn't exactly overjoyed to be spending his Saturday afternoon playing errand boy for Felix.

"Okay, well, I really will just be a minute. Come on in and take a load off." I gestured toward the sad loveseat and chair that constituted my tiny living room.

"Thanks."

He followed me into the apartment and sank into the chair while I put the flowers on the kitchen table. Then I hurried into my bedroom to put back on the dress and sandals I'd worn to brunch, swipe a lipstick across my mouth, and drag a brush through my hair. I slapped my sunglasses on my face and hung my purse over my arm.

"All set," I said brightly as I stepped into the living room.

His head was resting against the back of the small couch and his eyes were closed. At the sound of my voice, he snapped to attention.

"Wow. You're quick. Usually 'just a minute' means a solid hour—to a recording diva, at least," he said apologetically as he stood.

I nodded empathetically. "I get it. That's what it means to Amber, too." Then I caught myself. "I mean, that's what it *used* to mean."

He cocked his head. "Hey, wait a minute. You're the chef."

"Guilty as charged." Then I realized how close I'd come to being charged with murder and my cheeks burned at the poor choice of words. "Um, I mean, one and the same. Have we met?"

"No, I've just heard Felix and his father talking about you. You have an unusual name. It stuck."

"Oh." I decided it would be completely inappropriate to ask what the Patrick men had said about me, so I bit down on my lip to prevent the question from bursting out and probably chewed off my lipstick in the process. I headed for the door wondering what kind of date Felix had in mind.

Eleven

ELIX'S IDEA OF A PROPER date turned out to be a picnic spread, complete with a red-and-white checkered blanket and a bottle of chilled wine, at a Hollywood Bowl concert.

When we arrived at the Hollywood Bowl, Felix was waiting with a wicker picnic basket over his arm and a goofy smile pasted on his face. As I drew closer, I realized I recognized his expression—he was nervous, too. My stomach did a little flip.

As I exited the car in a ball of excitement, I awkwardly invited Marvin to join us because it felt weird to think that he'd be sitting in the car just waiting for me, but he declined.

"No, thanks. I don't care for jazz. Or soft cheese. I'll be happier in the car listening to my old school punk. You kids have fun," he said with a wink as he held the car door.

I smiled at Felix as I joined him at the curb. "Hi. Thanks for the flowers," I said.

He leaned in and kissed me right at my hairline above my ear. "You look great."

I flushed.

Marvin coughed discreetly. "I'll wait at the usual spot, Felix."

"Nah, go ahead and take off. I'll take Rosemary home," Felix said.

Oh. The little flip-flop morphed into a full-blown stomach roller coaster.

Marvin grinned and flashed him a thumbs up sign before getting back into the car. I pretended not to see it and tried to will myself not to blush. Turns out, that's not how physiological reactions work, and I could feel the heat rising on my face. Felix just laughed and grabbed my hand.

As we walked and talked, my awkwardness and discomfort sort of melted away. I know we ate and drank and was vaguely aware that music of some sort (jazz, if Marvin was to be trusted) was being played. But all that really registered was our conversation. He told me how he loved music—not just the popular hits that his dad's studio churned out—but all music, stretching back to baroque, classical, you name it. He'd been accepted at both Juilliard and Berklee College of Music as a piano student. But when he told his father his plans, Pat had exploded.

"He wouldn't even discuss it," Felix recounted. "He told me if I went to music school that was it. He'd disown me and cut me off. He told me I was going to UCLA to study business administration. So that's what I did." He reached over and tucked a strand of hair behind my ear with a wistful smile.

I thought my heart would crack right there in the middle of the crowd of people as his sadness washed over me.

"I'm sorry," I said, not knowing what else to say. I took his hand and laced my fingers through his. My pale freckled skin contrasted with his tanned, strong fingers.

"Don't be. One day, I'll take over the company, and, when I do, I'll change the direction completely. Instead of hip-hop crap, I'll produce serious music." He said it with all the conviction of a twenty-two-year old who's never had to consider the realities of the market.

His idealism made me feel ancient. The long months of reviewing the resort's balance sheets and coming up with increasingly desperate promotions to keep that sinking ship afloat had left me cynical.

"I hope your family business works out better than mine," I blurted without stopping to think about what I was saying.

Curiosity sparked in his eyes. "You have a family business?"

After months of keeping a lid on my disastrous, dysfunctional family, the whole pathetic story came pouring out. When I finished, my cheeks were wet with tears I hadn't even realized I'd shed.

"Hey, shh, it's okay," he soothed as he scooched across the blanket and snugged me into the crook of his arm. He pulled me tight and hugged me hard against his warm arm and side. Then he tipped my chin back and very, very gently, with a feather's touch, wiped away my tears. I took a deep, ragged breath and twisted my mouth into an approximation of a smile.

And then he covered my mouth with his.

I inhaled in surprise and tasted wine and salt. Part of my mind was racing, processing the fact that after all his flirting and innuendo, Felix Patrick was *kissing* me. But most of my mind was spinning with desire and pleasure. I wrapped my fingers around the dark curls at the base of his head and kissed him back with an urgency that surprised me. Time must have passed but it didn't feel that way. I felt suspended in that moment.

My arms slid down around his neck. He rested a hand on the small of my back and tipped me back so that I was reclining on the blanket and knelt over me. My heart thudded in my chest and electricity raced up my spine. He paused to take a breath and I opened my eyes to find his green eyes locked on mine with an intensity that made my skin hot.

"Wow," I whispered, my lips brushing his as I spoke.

"You can say that again," he said as he trailed a finger along the hollow where my throat met my clavicle.

I shivered. "Wow," I repeated with a grin as his lips pressed against mine.

~ ~ ~ ~ ~ ~ ~ ~ ~ ~

Somehow Felix didn't wreck his Porsche driving me home. I'm honestly not sure how he managed that feat—between the kisses he stole at every stop sign, red light, and pause in traffic and the fact that he had one hand on the steering wheel and the other firmly clasping my left hand, his thumb tracing circles on mine. Now, to be clear, I didn't exactly discourage this behavior. In my defense, though, I was giddy, grinning like a little kid and bouncing in my seat.

We didn't talk much during the long drive from the Hollywood Bowl to my apartment. I didn't mind the silence. Intelligent conversation was pretty much out of my grasp at the moment. I kept stealing sidelong glances at him as we inched along in Los Angeles' ever-present, excruciating traffic. Every time I looked over at him, he was already looking at me.

"Hey, there," he said as he caught me peeking at him when we were stopped at the traffic light at the end of my block.

Suddenly, I felt inexplicably shy. "Hey." I lowered my gaze.

He leaned over and cupped my face in his hands. He kissed me, hard and fast. My back arched and I strained against the seatbelt, my body yearning for his.

The driver behind us gave a short, polite honk. I opened one eye.

"The light's green," I said against his lips.

"I don't care." He pressed his mouth against mine.

The driver behind us laid on the horn like he meant it. I jumped back and pulled away while Felix laughed. He shook his head at me and slowly rolled through the intersection.

"You're terrible," I told him.

"Why do you care so much what other people think?" He asked like he was genuinely curious.

"What do you mean?" I stalled.

"This dude behind us, for instance. You're never going to see him again. What do you care if he's pissed that I made him wait thirty seconds so I could kiss the irresistible woman next to me?"

I considered the question. "I guess it's because I grew up as one of those weird, homeschooled sisters named after the herbs. I was always hyperconscious of what people in town thought of us," I said.

"You're not a little girl anymore, Rosemary. Don't worry about what people think of you. It's none of your business."

I didn't say what I was thinking, which was that it was easy enough to be so cavalier when you were the only son of a Hollywood power broker. Instead, I "hmmed" noncommittally.

He pulled into the fifteen-minute loading zone spot in front of my building, turned on his hazards, and killed the engine. "I'll walk you up."

I let myself out slowly, trying to think of a way to invite him in that didn't sound slutty.

Don't worry so much about what people think of you, I chided myself.

I waited on the sidewalk until he joined me beside the car. He immediately reached for my hand. "I had a great time," he said.

"Me, too." I swallowed and tried to work up some saliva in my suddenly dry throat. "Do you want to come up for a drink?" I said in what was supposed to be a casual tone. It sounded strained to me.

He stopped at the top of the stairs and leaned against the wall beside the intercom. He pulled me toward him. "I would love to come up—and not for a drink."

He kissed me hungrily, and my lips parted. His tongue darted into my mouth, exploring and probing. I pressed against him and made a noise that sounded embarrassingly like a kitten being strangled. When I could breathe, I rested my palms on his chest and looked up at him, about to reiterate the invitation was for a drink only.

"Then I think you'd better not come up."

Disappointment warred with longing in his eyes. I started to step away.

Felix grabbed my waist and held me still. "Don't do that. I like you, Rosemary. I like you a lot."

"And?" I breathed.

"And right now, I want you." His voice was a growl.

I felt my heart beating in my throat. "But?" I whispered.

"But I'm going to want you tomorrow and the day after that. And the day after that. So I'm going to kiss you good night like a gentleman and ask you to see me again." His eyes grew dark and heavy-lidded.

"You'll see me at your house. I work there, remember?"

"I mean after work."

"Another proper date?" I said, my mouth curving into a smile.

"Exactly."

"Okay."

"Great. Think about what you want to do for our next date. Now about that good night kiss ..." He trailed off and tangled his fingers in my hair, kissing my lips, my neck, the base of my throat.

"Very gentlemanly," I managed.

His tongue danced across the skin of my bare shoulder and I shivered. He lifted my hand and kissed it then bowed in an exaggerated gesture. He left me laughing on the front stairs to my apartment building. I sagged against the wall, grinning like an absolute idiot, and watched him walk back to his car. Then I pressed a hand to my tender, bruised lips and floated into the building and up the stairs to call Sage and squeal at her about my date.

Twelve

WE FELL INTO A PATTERN. I'd go to the Patrick mansion every morning, just like I used to when Amber was alive. But instead of juicing beets and assembling micro-green salads, I sourced local meats and fish for Pat, Antonio, and Felix. Although being freed from Amber's dietary restrictions allowed me to unleash my creativity in the kitchen, cooking for Pat was awkward. He posted bond (of course—I mean, I can't imagine how many zeroes the number would have to have to be out of his reach) but didn't return to the house. He was staying with Antonio just down the road. According to his statements to the press, the two were relieved and overjoyed that they could finally go public with their relationship, even though the news had cost

Antonio his body spray contract. I suspected the real reason they were shacking up had more to do with the frosty relationship between Pat and Felix than with the romance between Pat and Antonio. But as long as my salary kept being direct deposited into my bank account, I was happy to cook for him.

Antonio would zip up in one of his sports cars at eight a.m., noon, and seven p.m. and idle his engine loudly in the driveway while Alayna ran out whatever meal I'd boxed up for him and Pat. Felix usually made himself scarce until Antonio left. Then Felix would appear in the kitchen, steal a few kisses, and try to convince me to eat with him. I tried to explain that I didn't want to further blur the lines between my job and our budding relationship, but he was relentless. He made the point that it was lonely for him, all alone in the big house. So I conceded to join him—provided that he invited Alayna, too. He rolled his eyes at that but dutifully asked her to join us before each meal.

Every once in a while she'd deign to eat with us—usually when I'd prepared one of her favorites. Most of the time, she declined and muttered some version of 'poor little rich boy with no friends' once Felix was out of earshot. Her veiled hostility toward him struck me. He'd said she hated men, but it seemed as if she mainly hated him. It was an attitude I hadn't noticed before Felix and I became involved.

But then there were lots of things I'd failed to observe B.F. (before Felix). Things like the abundance of hidden nooks scattered throughout his family's home, all of which were perfectly suited to a quick session of nuzzling, caressing, and, of course, kissing. Felix was the best kisser whose lips I'd ever encountered. He left poor Thor the podiatrist in the dust. Another thing I hadn't noticed was how strong his arms were. I'd be pureeing the base for a gazpacho or dicing potatoes for a low country boil and suddenly he'd be pressed up against me, his arms encircling me tightly from behind. Anyway, what I'm trying to say is that in the days and weeks after our first proper date, the world seemed new and strange to me. All of my senses were heightened. Colors were brighter. Sounds were louder. Food tasted stronger. Smells were sharper. And touch—all he had to do was trail a finger down my arm or brush against my hip when we passed in the hallway, and my breath would catch and my knees would threaten to buckle.

I tried explaining this to Sage and Thyme on our monthly conference call to discuss the resort's dismal financial condition.

"I think you're in love," Thyme said in her serious psychology student voice.

"What? I'm not —"

Sage broke in. "Or in lust."

I sputtered a protest they couldn't possibly have heard over their combined laughter.

"Are you still going on your *proper* dates?" Thyme asked once she was able to breathe again.

"Um, well, yeah," I admitted. As a mater of fact, we were. Since the jazz concert at the Hollywood Bowl, we'd gone to a Lakers game (courtside), attended the opening of a Spanish restaurant, bowled at some retro hipster bowling alley, and represented the recording label at a fancy silent auction fundraiser. Each date had ended the same way: with us making out in a frenzy in front of my building, and me gently refusing to let Felix come upstairs. At this point, I imagined the people who lived directly across the street were viewing us as free entertainment.

"And you *still* haven't boned?" Sage asked in disbelief.

Boned? I felt the heat creep up my face. Although Sage and Thyme always shared the intimate details of their personal lives with me and one another, I was intensely private—even with my sisters.

"No." I hoped my tone made clear that this wasn't a subject I wanted to elaborate on.

No such luck.

"Maybe he's gay like his dad?" Thyme ventured.

The image of Felix pressed against me, his hands and mouth urgently roaming my body, flashed in my mind. "He's not gay," I said faintly.

"Then what's with all the proper dates?" Thyme said.

I was about to explain for the hundredth time that I just wanted to take it slow. I was a family employee. And according to the staff scuttlebutt, he could be a bit of a playboy. I didn't need a messy heartbreak. But I never had a chance to get the words out, because Sage offered her own theory.

"Maybe he thinks you're a virgin?" Sage suggested.

Before I could even respond, Thyme gasped. "Maybe she is. Are you, Rosie?"

"What? No."

"Oh, not Thor. Tell us it wasn't Thor," Sage said. The two of them burst into uncontrollable laughter again.

"That's it. This conversation is over," I said firmly in my oldest sister voice before changing the subject to something slightly less mortifying. "Have you reviewed the most recent P & L statements from the accountant?"

Thirteen

THE NEXT MORNING AT WORK, Felix turned up in the kitchen in his swim trunks while I was whipping up two frittatas—one for us and one for Pat and Antonio. He scanned the room, no doubt looking for Alayna.

"She's in the laundry room," I said.

He grinned and crossed the room in a hurry. "Good morning, beautiful." He planted a warm kiss on the nape of my neck.

"Mmmm. Morning," I managed, acutely aware of his mostly naked body about two inches from my non-naked one. I kept my eyes on the eggs.

He spun me around to face him.

"Are you free tonight?" he asked in a low voice as he wrapped his arms around my waist and pulled me toward him.

I swallowed hard. "Let's see." I pretended to think for a few seconds before smiling up at him. "Yep, free. What do you have in mind for tonight's proper date?"

Although I didn't think it was possible to get any closer than we already were, he pulled me even tighter. I could feel the heat rising from his bare chest. His voice grew husky, and he caressed the small of my back before his hands rested on my hips. "Well I've been thinking. We'd have five proper dates. I thought maybe tonight, we could do something quieter. I'd offer to make you dinner, but you're the pro. How does dinner for two at the apartment in Santa Monica sound?"

My pulse quickened at the thought of spending a whole evening alone with him, out of sight of public eyes. I wet my lips. "Sounds great. I'll go grocery shopping after work. Meet you there at eight?"

"I'll pick you up."

He ran his hands through my hair. I pulled his head down toward mine. His lips met mine, salty and openmouthed.

"You have no idea how crazy you drive me," he said.

I uttered a wordless sound before he covered my mouth again. I leaned back against the counter and he moved his lips down my throat and ran his hands along my body. I arched, quivering.

A door banged shut. We both jumped at the loud sound and pulled apart guiltily. I opened my eyes expecting to see Alayna glaring at us with her arms full of towels and sheets. Instead, Antonio Santos stood awkwardly in the doorway, a faint smirk playing on his lips.

"I knocked. I guess you didn't hear me." He raised his right eyebrow.

"I guess not," Felix agreed in a strangled voice.

I smoothed a hand over my hair and tried to form a thought so that I could possibly form words. What I came up with was both rude and defensive-sounding. "What are you doing here?"

Antonio's left eyebrow joined his right at his hairline.

"Sorry. I mean, you've never come into the house before. And you're early. Breakfast isn't ready," I said in a rush, tripping over myself to clarify what I meant. After all, he was Pat's significant other. I really didn't need to lose my job over a perceived slight.

"I can see that you're running a bit late this morning, eh?" he asked as the smirk returned.

I blushed and turned away, busying myself with the ingredients to get the blasted frittata into the pan already.

"To answer the question," Antonio said to my back, "I was hoping to have a chance to talk to your boyfriend. Felix, a word?"

Beside me, Felix stiffened. "We don't have anything to talk about."

"Actually, we do. I love your father. And he loves you. It's time to stop this silent treatment. You're hurting him." Antonio pressed on as though he wasn't the least bit perturbed by Felix's discomfort or rising anger. Of course, a man who made his living driving a little car around a track at high speeds probably had sufficient testosterone to weather a showdown with just about anyone.

"This is none of your business."

"You're wrong. I love Pat—that makes it my business whether you like it or not."

I sneaked a peek at Felix. His mouth was a hard, angry slash and he was clenching and relaxing his fists rhythmically. The hair on his bare arms stood up.

Oh, man.

If this was going to escalate, I didn't want to be a witness to it. I cleared my throat. "This frittata can wait. Why don't I step into the library and give you two some privacy?"

"Thank you," Antonio said at the same time that Felix barked, "No."

I stifled a sigh.

"No," Felix repeated. "Anything you have to say to me, you can say in front of Rosemary. I'll give you two minutes. Clock's running."

I forced myself to concentrate on assembling breakfast and to ignore the tension between the two men.

"If that's the way you want to do this, fine. You have to know your father didn't kill Amber. So why the cold shoulder, huh? Is it because you disapprove of our relationship?"

"Please. I don't give two craps about his personal life. Whatever makes him happy. I mean, why would I pass judgment on my dad when he's always been *so supportive* of me and my dreams. Like when I told him I got into Julliard. He was so proud of me ... Oh, wait." Felix's words were laced with bitter sarcasm.

"Felix," Antonio said in a low, kind voice, "can't you put the past aside? Your dad needs you."

From the corner of my eye, I watched as Felix's face grew increasingly redder. After a long moment, he jutted his chin and said, "If he needed me, he'd have come here himself. But the thing you don't seem to understand about your boyfriend is that he doesn't *need* anybody. *You* need to stop meddling." He turned to me and snarled, "I'll be in my room. Let me know when Speed Racer's gone and my breakfast is ready."

As he stomped out of the kitchen, I pushed down the sting from the way he spoke to me. Once I could manage a wobbly grin, I faced Antonio. "Do you want a cup of coffee while you wait for your food?"

"I'd love that," he said with a hint of his trademark sexy smolder. But his dark eyes were subdued.

~ ~ ~ ~ ~ ~ ~ ~ ~ ~

After Antonio left, I waited until Alayna headed out to run errands and then went upstairs to Felix's room. I stood for a moment in the hall, gathering my thoughts, before rapping lightly on his closed bedroom door. The heavy bass line of his dad's label's latest hit was audible through the door.

A few seconds later, the music switched off and the door swung open. Felix had traded his swim trunks for a pair of low-slung jeans but hadn't bothered to put on a shirt. I kept my gaze away from his shirtless torso and pinned my eyes on his face.

"Your breakfast is ready," I said stiffly.

As I turned to go, he caught my wrist. "Hey, come on. Don't be that way."

I gave him a long look. He sighed, slumping his shoulders. I waited to see if he'd apologize for his behavior in the kitchen.

When he didn't, I took a centering breath then said, "I didn't like the way you talked to me downstairs—not as an employee and definitely not as ... a whatever I am to you." My voice sounded shaky and I was burning with embarrassment at having to tiptoe around the issue of our relationship status, but I felt good about standing up for myself. Even if it ended up meaning the end of our ... whatever it was.

I moved to shake my wrist loose of his hand, but he shook his head. "No. Don't go. Stay here and talk to me." He released my wrist and put his hands on the doorframe, one of each side of me. "You're not my employee. You happen to work for my dad, but you're my girlfriend, or at least I hope you are." The color of his eyes deepened with an intensity that made my breath catch in my throat.

Girlfriend? The word echoed in my mind.

He didn't move to touch me but my traitorous body reacted as if he had, quivering and yielding. I forced myself to ignore my physical reaction and said, "Not if you think you can talk to me like you did in the kitchen, I'm not."

The beginning of a laugh escaped his mouth, but he must have belatedly realized I wasn't joking because the sound died almost instantly. He gave me what I can only describe as a wounded look. "You're really mad about that, aren't you?"

"I am. You need to be more careful about how you treat people," I said, cringing a little at my lecturing tone. But, I figured, in for a dime, in for a dollar, so I pressed on. "And that goes for your dad as well as for me."

His eyes widened in shock that I'd side with Antonio but before he had a chance to respond, Alayna called up the stairs. "Rosemary? Are you up there? The policeman is here looking for you."

Felix blinked at that news, and I imagine I did, too. I shot him a look that said our conversation was far from over and headed down the main staircase to the front of the house wondering what Detective Drummond wanted to harass me about now.

I didn't have long to wonder. As I was descending the stairs, he was already yapping at me.

"I didn't realize there was a second-floor kitchen in this place," he said dryly.

I smiled in what I hoped was a mysterious way to show that his needling didn't affect me. "What can I do for you, detective?"

He switched on his cop voice. "I wanted to let you know the district attorney is going to subpoena you."

"What? Why me?" Panic was rising in my throat.

"Take it easy. It's routine. You've seen Roland Patrick lose his temper on multiple occasions. The prosecutors are building a case that he's a volatile man, prone to outbursts and capable of murder. They'll want you to testify about your experiences as a household employee." He gestured with a rolled-up piece of paper in his hands for emphasis. I figured that was the subpoena.

I gripped the bannister. "But ... I ... Has Alayna been subpoenaed, too? She's worked here longer than I have. They should talk to her."

"What's the matter, Rosemary? You and your boyfriend think Mr. Patrick did it, don't you?"

I narrowed my eyes and shot back. "Never mind what I think. I thought *you* said he's not guilty. You're just going to railroad an innocent man?"

Anger sparked in his eyes. I was on quite a roll with pissing people off today.

"I have to work the case. Patrick maintains his innocence. And Antonio Santos hounds me just about daily insisting we've got the wrong guy. But I don't have any other viable suspects at this point. And, since your boyfriend won't talk to me and hasn't leapt forward to defend his father, my hands are effectively tied."

"Hmm. Protect and serve, eh?"

His face was a stony mask but he didn't react. Instead he said in a casual voice, "I see you're no longer denying that Felix Patrick is your boyfriend. It must be weird to know that you're dating a guy whose dad is probably going to do time for murder."

My stomach dropped thinking about it. As glad as I was that I was no longer the prime suspect, I couldn't help feeling just the teensiest bit bad for Pat. I pursed my lips and thought about how to say what I wanted Detective Drummond to hear.

"Listen, I don't speak for Felix, but I really don't think he believes his father killed Amber. He's just ... mad at him about some other stuff and doesn't want to talk to him or help him out." I realized as I said the words that I was making Felix sound like a total dirtbag.

Detective Drummond apparently agreed because he raised an eyebrow and gave a low, long whistle. "Wow. That kid's a real peach, huh?" He paused and shot me a meaningful look before continuing. "Unless, of course, he actually benefits from his father taking the fall."

This again. I was about to remind him that we'd already been through this and I wasn't amused, when something about the way he'd said it this time piqued my curiosity.

"Benefits? How do you mean? Like, financially?"

He shrugged. "As it turns out, he would benefit financially, according to our forensic accounting folks. But I was thinking more immediately. If Felix killed his stepmother, then it's definitely not in his interest to help his father clear his name. Better to manufacture some lame family feud to explain his silence. It's clever, really."

"Oh, so this is the same old song and dance as before. You don't have any *actual* reason to suspect Felix."

"The murderer tried to frame you, in case you've forgotten. Felix Patrick had the same access to the kitchen as his dad did. And you told me he called Amber a whore the day she died. Means, motive, and opportunity are all there. Then, all of a sudden, he's not speaking to his father *and* has this big romantic interest in you. That effectively sets up his dad and neutralizes you as a witness. Pretty convenient."

I stared at him in disbelief. "You're describing a ... sociopath or something." Felix would never do the things Detective Drummond was suggesting. Never. Not to mention this little theory meant Felix was just using me. No way. He couldn't be faking the heat between us. Could he?

"More like a psychopath," Detective Drummond said. "Psychopaths can be very charming."

"He's not a psychopath or a sociopath or any other kind of path," I hissed. I twisted my neck and peered up the stairs, worried that Felix would overhear this utterly insane conversation.

When I turned back to Detective Drummond, he was watching me with this sad, knowing expression.

"Here," he said, handing me the subpoena and his business card.

"I already have your card."

"I know. But I wrote my cell phone number on this one. When the time comes and you need it, call me. Any time, day or night."

"If the time comes, you mean," I corrected him but slipped the card into my pocket.

He opened his mouth to say something but clamped it closed as if he'd thought the better of it. He touched two fingers to his forehead in a salute and then turned to let himself out.

He looked back with his hand on the doorknob and gave me another sad look. "Be careful, please. I'd hate it if something happened to you." His voice hitched. Before I could respond, he was out the door.

I headed back upstairs, but when I got to Felix's bedroom, it was empty. From the hall window, I watched as his car pulled out of the garage and zipped along behind Detective Drummond's Crown Victoria, down the hill, and out of sight.

So much for our first improper date.

Fourteen

AT EIGHT O'CLOCK, I was curled up on my lumpy excuse for a couch with a bottle of red wine, a container of Trader Joe's dark chocolate pretzels, and an extra-large portion of self-pity. The plan was to wile away the hours watching cooking shows, so I could at least pretend that I was doing something marginally productive. The first time the intercom buzzed, I ignored it—mainly because Alton Brown was midway through his explanation of brining. I just love the way that guy marries science and food. The second time, whoever was downstairs leaned insistently on the button effectively drowning out my stand-in date.

I harrumphed my way over to the button. "Who is it?"

Felix's voice was conciliatory even through the static. "It's your very sorry boyfriend. Please may I come up?"

I nearly choked on my pretzel, but luckily, I still had my glass in my hand. I took a big gulp of syrah to wash it down and sputtered, "Um, sure." I buzzed him in and then raced wildly through my apartment, clicking off the television with a silent apology to my boy Alton.

I tore through my closet in search of a cute, casual outfit that Felix hadn't seen yet and settled on a filmy cream-colored tank top and a flouncy skirt. I tossed my tee shirt and sweats on the bed and hurried to pull on the dressier clothes. I brushed my teeth with my right-hand while pulling a comb through my hair with my left. I ran a lipstick across my mouth and slipped my feet into my sandals, then hightailed it back to the kitchen and grabbed a second wine glass. I refilled my glass and poured one for Felix, then leaned against the counter, panting to catch my breath. For the first time ever, I was grateful that my building's ancient elevator took its groaning time moving from floor to floor.

My heart rate had slowed almost to normal by the time Felix knocked on my apartment door. I exhaled and walked over to answer the door, trying to keep my nerves in check.

I unlocked the door and swung it open. "Hi," I said, standing aside to let him in.

"Hi yourself, gorgeous." He moved toward me like he was planning to kiss me, but I closed the door and evaded him by heading for the galley kitchen.

"Wine?" I asked, picking up both glasses and extending one toward him.

Uncertainty flashed in his eyes as if he'd just realized this wasn't going to be quite as easy as he'd assumed. *Good,* I thought, sipping my wine. *Gah.* Freshly brushed teeth and red wine were not a winning combination. I managed to convert my grimace into a smile.

"Uh, thanks." He reached for the glass. "To makeup sex. The best kind there is," he said, raising the glass toward me to toast.

I pinned him with a frosty look and took another drink, concentrating hard on not imagining what he had in mind.

He waited for a second, realized I wasn't going to toast or respond, and then rested his glass on the counter.

He closed the distance between us. "Rosemary, I'm sorry. I'm sorry I snapped at you in the kitchen. I'm sorry I reacted the way I did when you came upstairs to talk. I'm just ... really sorry. There's no excuse for the way I treated you." His voice dripped with sincerity and his chiseled face wore an expression of pain.

My anger melted. Not just because he apologized, but also because I thought about all he'd been through recently. Although no one was exactly mourning Amber, her murder had been a shock. His father's relationship, another shock. His father's arrest for murder, yet another. And even his crappiness toward his dad was the result of his own hurt about having to give up music school.

"Apology accepted," I breathed. I put my wineglass down, raised myself on my tiptoes, and wrapped my arms around his neck, pulling his head down so his full lips met mine. Detective Drummond's warning echoed in my mind, but I swatted it away like the annoying insect it was and let my euphoria wash over me.

After a long, long kiss that tasted like wine (and I hoped no toothpaste), Felix pulled back and searched my eyes.

"Good. Now that we've settled that, will you still come over to the apartment?"

I swiveled and scanned the room. What was wrong with my place? Shabby, cramped, and dated though it may be, it *was* habitable.

He must have sensed what I was thinking, because he flashed me a lopsided grin. "I had Alayna pick up some food and deliver it to the apartment for me. If you're still willing to cook, we can have dinner in the garden and then ..." His voice trailed off and his eyes traced my body.

"Sounds great," I croaked through dry lips, my pulse hammering in my ear. I even ignored the fact that he'd sent the maid to do the grocery shopping, and I'd have no control over the menu.

"Good." He took my hand and led me to the door. I grabbed my handbag on my way out.

As we waited for the elevators, our fingers interlaced and our hips brushing, he leaned over and whispered in my ear, "Your shirt is on inside out."

What? My eyes darted down to the front of the spaghetti strap tank. It looked fine to me.

"It's raw-seamed," I explained. "That means the seams aren't finished. I guess it's trendy."

"Your tag is on the outside, too," he countered gently, reaching a hand under my hair to tug on the tag. I shivered at the touch of his hand on my back.

"Oh."

The elevator doors opened, and we stepped inside. My face burned. *Smooth, Rosemary. Really smooth.*

He followed me into the car with a smirk. "Don't worry about it. You won't be wearing it much longer."

~ ~ ~ ~ ~ ~ ~ ~ ~ ~

It felt weird to be back at the apartment after the whole Pat and Antonio / police scenario. The rooms felt closed up and smelled slightly musty, even though some-one—Alayna, probably—had opened some windows and turned on the old-fashioned paddle-style ceiling fans.

"Hasn't anybody used this place since, um, that night?" I asked as I rifled through the produce and sea-food in the fridge.

"No. We just haven't had a need," he said. As he passed by me with a box of kitchen matches and a hand-ful of candles, he gave my behind a playful bump with his hip and I pitched forward into the fridge.

"Hey, watch it!" I protested in mock outrage. But he was already gone, out on the patio, lighting candles, turning on the music, and generally setting the stage for a night of romance.

Involuntarily, I glanced toward the door to the bed-room just off the kitchen. The door was ajar, and I could see candlelight flickering off the windows behind the king bed. A soft bedside light shined on the bed, high-lighting the blue and silver bed linens. I started to feel warm and stuck my head back in the fridge for a mo-ment to get myself under control.

Felix wandered back in. "Can you make something out of what's in there?"

I closed the refrigerator door and turned to face him, smoothing my skirt over my hips in a nervous gesture.

"Sure. We've got scallops, avocado, limes, heirloom tomatoes, and a jalapeño. I can make a nice ceviche. Or I can cook the Arborio rice in the cabinet and make a seafood risotto, if you want something more substantial."

A lazy smile played across his lips. "Let's go with the ceviche. I think a light meal's called for. Plus it won't take so long to get to dessert."

I hadn't noticed any ingredients that would work to create a dessert, but I had a feeling I knew what he had in mind. I gathered my ingredients and headed for the butcher block island in the middle of the room.

I concentrated on squeezing limes and dicing tomatoes. He busied himself making a pitcher of margaritas. We worked in comfortable silence—the only sounds were the rhythmic thud of my knife against the cutting surface and the faint strains of the music wafting in from the garden patio. I was glad for the lack of conversation. My body was a live wire. I was buzzing with excitement, nervousness, and anticipation.

He placed two glasses with salted rims on the island, stood behind me, and slipped his cool hands under my top, resting them on my warm stomach. I started at his touch and nearly dropped my knife. His hands spanned my body, tight around my waist.

"You feel hot. Maybe we should eat inside. I can close the windows and turn on the air conditioning."

"No," I said too quickly. "The patio's fine. It's a beautiful night."

He nuzzled my bare shoulder. "Mmm. Sultry."

I didn't know if he meant me or the evening, so I let that go unanswered. I got to work assembling the ceviche and arranging the tomato-avocado relish on top while he got to work running his tongue over the nape of my neck. His hands were dancing across my torso, up, down, always teasing.

I inhaled sharply. My knees were made of jelly. I swallowed hard and leaned forward against the island for support. I eyed the margarita. I'm well passed the stage of life where fueling myself with liquid courage seemed smart. But I was going to pass out before we ate if I didn't settle my nerves somehow. I reached for the glass and took a long drink. Salty, sweet, bitter. The liquid rolled down my throat, and I rolled my spine back like I was in Pilates class, bumping right up against his hard thighs and taut chest. He gripped my hips and held me tight.

I swallowed hard. "I'm nearly done here. Why don't you wait outside on the patio?"

He held me for another long moment then released me. "Good idea," he said in a strained voice. Then he scooped his drink up from the island and left the kitchen without another word.

I waited until I gained sufficient control of my movements that I was reasonably sure I could slice the fleshy scallops without cutting myself. Then I raced through the final steps of preparing the ceviche and left the dish to marinate on the counter for fifteen minutes or so. My hands were still shaking slightly when I lifted my glass and headed out to the patio to join Felix.

~ ~ ~ ~ ~ ~ ~ ~ ~

I was too keyed up to do much more than pick at my dinner, but Felix ate like a starving man—or a man in a hurry. He shoveled the ceviche into his mouth like he was being timed, pausing only to take a few gulps of his drink.

"That was amazing," he said when he finished, pushing away the cocktail glass I'd used as a serving dish.

"Thanks," I said.

"I mean it. You're really talented."

I smiled modestly and decided not to tell him that ceviche was one of those big-bang dishes that are super-easy to prepare but have a huge impact. Instead I dabbed my lips with my napkin and pushed back my chair. During our short meal, I'd managed to get a grip on my nerves. Something about the fragrant garden air, the gentle sound of the fountain water tinkling over the rocks, and the soft jazz music soothed me enough to replace my nervousness with sheer anticipation.

"I don't know about you, but I'm ready for dessert," I said boldly as I pushed back my chair and stood.

His eyes widened, and he crossed the patio to join me. He stared down at me for a moment that seemed to stretch on forever.

"Oh, I'm ready for dessert," he said throatily.

I smiled up at him.

What happened next is seared in my mind in slow motion. He lowered his head toward mine. Then, when his face was just inches from mine, he pitched forward and his stomach gurgled loudly, sloshily. His face stretched, contorting in horror and pain, and his Adam's apple seemed to jump in his throat.

Somehow, I *knew* and managed to squirm away from him, jerking to my left just as an arc of vomit poured out of his mouth.

"Ahh," I gagged. Other people's puke always made me puke, too. It was some kind of reflex thing. I raced for the bathroom.

After I lost my dinner, I rinsed my mouth with the mouthwash someone had helpfully left on the sink. Once I felt somewhat human, I slinked back outside to check on Felix. I expected him to be mortified or, at least, embarrassed. Instead, he was immobile on the cobblestone, face down in a pool of tequila and half-digested scallops.

With bile rising again in my own throat, I hurried to roll him onto his back. "Felix!" I shouted.

He groaned and tried to raise his head off the ground but didn't seem to be able to.

Fear crowded out my disgust, and I grabbed him by both shoulders and shook him, calling his name. His eyes met mine registering understanding but he didn't respond, and when I let go of him gently, he fell back, limp and still. I caught his head before it bounced off the hard stone and eased it back then raced to the kitchen to grab my purse, dug out my cell phone, and dialed 911 with trembling fingers.

"Nine-one-one. What's your emergency?" A calm female voice said immediately after the first ring.

"My boyfriend's sick. He vomited and now he seems to be paralyzed or something!" I blurted out frantically as I hurried back to the patio.

"Has he been doing drugs?"

"What? No. No, listen, there's something wrong. I think he's really sick." I took a frantic look at Felix. His chest rose and fell with each shallow breath he took. His breathing seemed labored, but at least he was breathing. His Roman brow was slick with sweat, and he was pale, almost gray, under his tan.

"Has he been drinking alcohol?"

"He's had a margarita. Maybe two. That's not it, okay? Please—"

"Ma'am, I'm going to help you. I just have to determine if we're dealing with a possible overdose," the operator assured me evenly.

"I understand." I took a ragged breath. "He didn't overdose. He's a perfectly healthy twenty-two-year old.

We just finished dinner and he got sick. I went to the bathroom to ... um, clean up. When I got back to him, he was just laying there. It looks like he's having trouble breathing."

"Okay, ma'am. What's the street address?"

I had no idea. I took another look at Felix, who hadn't moved, and raced to the front of the house.

"Ma'am?"

"I'm sorry, I'm still here," I shouted into the phone, while I pawed through a stack of glossy magazines looking for an address label. The way my hands shook made it harder than it should have been but I found the address and rattled off the house number and street then listened to the clacking of keys on the other end of the phone.

After a moment she spoke in that same calm voice. "An ambulance is en route. In the meantime, I need you to make sure his airway is clear."

"Give me a minute."

I ran back outside and tried to catch my breath. She walked me through the steps and stayed on the line while I opened Felix's mouth and checked his airway, managing not to gag in the process. His skin was clammy and he still wasn't moving. But his eyes were open. I could see his fear.

"It's going to be okay," I promised him. His face twitched as if he was trying to smile.

The 911 operator offered to keep the line open until the EMTs arrived, but I thanked her and hung up. I had another call to make. I reached for my purse again and dumped the contents on the table. I dug through the pile—lipstick, keys, emergency dark chocolate bar— there it was. I dialed the number scrawled on Detective Drummond's business card and waited for him to pick up.

"Drummond," he said after the first ring.

"It's Rosemary. I need your help."

Fifteen

I WAS SITTING IN THE waiting room of the emergency department at the UCLA Medical Center alternately wringing my hands about Felix and wondering if the scent of barf was clinging to me or if it was just my imagination when the doors whooshed open and loud footsteps hurried toward me from outside. I looked up hoping to see Detective Drummond. No such luck. It was Pat and Antonio. I stood up.

"How is he?" Antonio said when they were still five or six feet away.

"I don't know. They won't let me go back because I'm not family and no one's come out with an update. But, he was in pretty bad shape when they took him back."

Pat gave me a look that made me think I definitely did smell like vomit. I forced myself not to look away.

"I'm sorry," I said simply. For all his parenting mistakes, he was still Felix's father. And I imagined his barely controlled rage was covering up a lot of fear and panic.

He didn't bother to respond. Instead, he stalked off to bark at an admission desk nurse, who ran around to the open the door and take him back to see his son.

Antonio and I stood in awkward silence for a moment. Well, we were silent. The room was filled with the sound of battling televisions—one was blaring "Family Feud" while the other was blasting an MSNBC financial news broadcast at full volume. It was like being in a dueling piano bar in one of the inner circles of hell.

He grimaced as the matriarch of the Argawal family shrieked with joy at her clan's successful steal from their opponent. Personally, I was delighted for her. During my time in the waiting room I'd come to loathe the Hampton family's smarmy father. Who could trust a guy wearing both a belt and suspenders?

"Are you okay?" Antonio asked gently.

I felt tears well up behind my eyes and kept my focus on the game show until I could trust myself to answer him without crying. "I'm fine. I just can't believe this happened."

Now *that* was an understatement. I'd planned to spend my night indulging all the Felix fantasies I'd stockpiled during our weeks of dating, not sitting on a sticky, no doubt germ-laden, plastic chair watching two families fight it out over their ability to guess what their fellow Americans were thinking while some guy in a suit was screaming about the stock exchange and buying gold. I had spent the first twenty minutes in a flurry of texting with my sisters but then my phone battery had died. It was a good thing I'd called Pat from the ambulance.

Antonio looked at me closely and I forced myself to stay stoic. Although I suspected collapsing into a soggy, sobbing mess in Antonio's arms would make me feel better, it wasn't going to help Felix. "Really, I'm fine," I reiterated.

"Okay. Good. Can you tell me what happened?" he asked in a low voice.

I gnawed on my top lip with my teeth and tried to come up with a reasonably sanitized, minimally humiliating version of the night's events. "We had dinner in ... at the, um, garden apartment." He averted his eyes at the mention of the apartment where his own romantic evening with Pat had been crashed by the cops. I went on, "After we ate, he got sick. I have this thing about people yakking—"

"You also get ill?"

I looked at him in surprise. "Yes."

"You're very empathetic, yes? A compassionate soul. My mother was the same way." His voice was gentle, almost reverent.

"Hmm." I didn't feel like getting into the science of mirror neurons at the moment, so I just nodded my agreement with a beatific smile.

"Go on. You got sick as well and then ..."

"I went back outside. Felix had collapsed on the patio. He was conscious but it was like he was paralyzed. He was just lying there, limp, and it seemed like he was having a hard time breathing. It was really odd and happened so suddenly. He didn't complain that he felt sick or anything. He was perfectly fine. And then, just like that, he wasn't."

He was more than fine, actually. He was revved up and ready to go. I decided to keep that detail to myself.

"I'm sorry that Pat was rude to you. He's just worried about his son."

"It's okay," I assured him. I felt a certain degree of magnanimity about the whole thing—yes, Felix was obviously really sick, and, yes, the night ranked as among the worst romantic nights in history, but I'd gotten him medical attention quickly, and, someday, we'd have a good laugh about it. I could afford to act generously in the face of Pat's unkindness.

I was just getting on a roll with my delusional optimism when two things happened to bring me back to earth and miserable reality.

One, Pat came back from the exam area flanked by two grim-faced, white-coated medical professionals and announced, "He's been poisoned." Everyone stared straight at me.

Two, right as Pat dropped his bombshell, Detective Drummond strolled in through the entrance.

~ ~ ~ ~ ~ ~ ~ ~ ~ ~

I stared out the rear passenger window of Detective Drummond's car not seeing anything. After some indeterminate period of time, I registered the fact that we weren't moving.

I leaned forward and wrapped my fingers through he wire cage that separated me from the front seat. "Why are we just sitting here?" I asked Detective Drummond.

He met my eyes in the rear view mirror and shook his head. "I'm trying to decide what to do with you."

That wasn't what I expected to hear. After the doctors had reported that Felix was suffering from food poisoning, which in their medical opinion was the clear result of inexpertly, if not negligently, prepared seafood, Pat had erupted. Purple-faced, he'd demanded that Detective Drummond arrest me. And Detective Drummond hadn't wasted any time in reciting the Miranda warning and hustling me out of the hospital waiting room and into the back seat of the car.

"Aren't you going to take me down to the station and throw me in some depressing, cramped room until your boss decides to come in and yell at me while she throws some metal chairs or something?" The image of Detective Sullivan hurtling furniture cheered me up enough that I managed a small grin.

"You're pretty cavalier for a woman who's been accused of poisoning her boyfriend," he said, raising an eyebrow. "Also, your blouse is on inside out."

I was past the point of being embarrassed by my clothing mishap. Narrowly avoiding being vomited on while making out apparently thickens a girl's skin. "I didn't accidentally poison Felix. Just like I didn't serve nuts to Amber. Believe it or not, I *am* a professional chef. I know what I'm doing in the kitchen. Anyway, am I under arrest or not?"

He shrugged. "I mainly wanted to get you out of there and away from Mr. Patrick. He doesn't seem to have the best handle on his temper. But, Rosemary, you need to understand that the mess this food poisoning business has put you in."

I stared blankly at him in the mirror.

He sighed and ran his hand through his hair, leaving spiky brown waves in his wake. "Who's been charged with killing Amber Patrick?" he asked in a put-upon, teacher's voice.

"Pat. Although you apparently think Felix did it. Or do you? I can't keep track."

He ignored that. "And who was our initial suspect?"

"I was."

"Right—because you were her chef, and you made her last meal. And now Felix is deathly ill after eating a meal you prepared."

"Hang on. My cooking didn't kill Amber. You *know* I didn't use nuts in that gravy. Someone poured peanut oil in her wine, remember? And Felix may have food poisoning—"

"Did you listen to anything those doctors said? Felix told them you made ceviche."

"So?"

"So you served him raw scallops, and twenty minutes later he was sick as a dog."

"First of all, ceviche isn't *raw*. The food is denatured. That means it's cooked in acid. It's completely safe. What I was going to say was, he may have food poisoning, but he *didn't* get it from eating my food." I could hear the indignation in my voice. "Maybe he got a bad burger or something when he was out this afternoon."

He knitted his eyebrows together in a worried vee. "Can you stop arguing with me long enough to focus? Surely you can see that you just displaced Pat as prime suspect again. Tell me you understand this. The facts may bear you out, but the way it looks .... Well, it looks bad for you."

"Wait a minute. What's this do to your pet theory? Do you think Felix poisoned himself to put me back in the hot seat?" I said it in an effort to show how absurd it was to think Felix had killed Amber. But as the words came out of my mouth, I started to wonder. Could he have? It seemed crazy but no more crazy than the fact that I was once again in police custody.

Apparently, Detective Drummond didn't think it was overly fantastical either, because his face took on a thoughtful expression and he was silent for a moment, considering it. Then he shook his head. "Doubtful. Too risky. What if he didn't get sick until after you left? He could have died."

I decided not to mention that our plans had called for me to spend the night. "Then who do you think did this? Pat?" I didn't see how Pat could have done it, given that his son hadn't given him the time of day since his arrest. And, as far as I know, Pat wasn't much of an actor. His worry in the waiting room had seemed real.

Detective Drummond started the engine and rolled the cruiser out of the parking lot. "I don't know. And until Felix's test results come back, I'm sorry, but we're going to have to operate under the assumption that you gave him food poisoning—accidentally or not."

I bit down so hard on my lower lip that I tasted blood. After a long pause, when I trusted myself to speak, I asked, "May I at least turn my shirt right side in before you parade me through the station and book me." *Book me?* I could hardly believe what I was saying.

He cleared his throat and kept his eyes on the traffic ahead. "I'm not taking you to the station. I'm taking you home."

We rode in silence across town. I don't know what he was thinking, but I was thinking my best move was to keep my mouth firmly shut so I didn't say anything to make him change his mind.

When we reached my apartment, I sat up straight, ready to spring out of the car as soon as it slowed to a stop. But when I reached for the door handle, duh, there wasn't one.

Detective Drummond killed the engine and walked around to open the door and let me out.

"Thanks," I mumbled.

"You're welcome." He waited until I raised my eyes to meet his gaze. "Do you want me to walk you up to your place?"

"Why?"

He shrugged. "I don't know. Even though you're an impossible pain in the ass, I sort of feel sorry for you. I just wanted to make sure you're okay."

Great. That's what every woman wants to hear. I'm so pathetic this hardened law enforcement officer pities me.

I squared my shoulders. "I'm fine. And I don't need your sympathy." I started to walk away with as much dignity I could muster, digging through my purse for my keys. I made it about a third of the way up the stairs before he called my name. I stopped and looked over my shoulder.

"This should go without saying, but don't leave town." His tone of voice was kind, but the words tore at me, highlighting just how upside-down my life had turned.

I just nodded that I understood and turned back around fast, before the tears that were threatening to fall could escape and humiliate me any further—if such a thing was even possible at this point.

Sixteen

THE NEXT SEVERAL DAYS WERE a tearful blur. I spent most of my time clinging to the phone, talking to whichever one of my sisters could spare the time to deal with me and my woes. I got the impression that Sage and Thyme had worked out between themselves a schedule for calling to check on me. Ordinarily, I'd chafe at being handled by my younger sisters, but this wasn't an ordinary situation. I was, not to put too fine a point on it, a complete mess.

Felix was still in the hospital but was expected to make a full recovery, at least according to Alayna, who was the only person associated with the Patrick family who was still speaking to me. Pat had sent a certified letter from his attorney, officially firing me. Felix had left instructions with the charge nurse on his floor that he didn't want to speak to me. Even Antonio, who I thought might be somewhat sympathetic to my situation, had tersely asked me to not to contact him again when I called him for an update.

On the afternoon of the fourth day of my self-imposed exile, even Alton Brown's voice was getting on my nerves and my craving for a bacon cheeseburger had reached epic proportions. So I found a big pair of sunglasses in my dresser—the kind a 1940s movie star might wear to evade her adoring fans—and ventured outside, blinking at the sunlight. I enjoyed the feeling of the sun warming my shoulders through the windows as I headed to the In-N-Out Burger.

I ordered at the drive-through window and ate my burger at a nearby park. I fed the edges of my bun to the gathered pigeons and sat on the bench soaking in a little more sun as I watched them. When I returned to the car, I fully intended to head back to my apartment but the Saab seem to have a mind of its own. Before I knew it, I was parking in the cracked and weed-choked abandoned lot behind Loving Hands.

I did a quick survey of the interior of my car to make sure nothing of any perceived value was visible before locking the doors. Then I squeezed through the busted-up chain link fence that surrounded the back of the shelter and slinked in the back door into the kitchen. As usual, Deb was running a one-woman show.

I coughed and knocked on the stainless steel shelving to announce my presence. "Hey."

She turned in the direction of my voice, wiping her hands on her stained apron. "Hey, yourself. Where've you been? You think people stop needing to eat just because you get yourself caught up in a Hollywood scandal?"

Well, that answered the question of whether Deb had heard about my most recent troubles. I pushed the sunglasses onto the top of my head and tried to think of a witty comeback. Instead, to my horror, I burst into tears.

Her face softened and she hurried around the counter. "Hey, hey, stop that. I was just kidding, I didn't mean to upset you," she said. She ripped off a rectangle of industrial unbleached paper towel and handed it to me.

I dabbed at my eyes with the sandpapery towel and sniffed, "I'm just so embarrassed."

"Embarrassed? You're famous! Do you have any idea how many people in this town would give their left boob to get as much press coverage as you've gotten in the past week?" she laughed.

I blew my nose into the rough paper towel and immediately regretted it. "I'm not famous, I'm notorious," I protested. I crumbled the paper towel into a ball and tossed it into the trashcan.

"Notorious, infamous, famous, whatever—this town thrives on celebrity. It's all the same." She was shaking her head at me.

"Can we talk about something else, please? Anything else."

"Sure. Make yourself useful while we talk." She handed me an eight-inch knife and directed me toward a mountain of baking potatoes.

There was something soothing about the act of slicing through the firm tubers. I established a constant rhythm with the knife and poured out the whole ugly story while I made short work of the pile. By the time I finished telling her about my unemployment and police surveillance, I had a heaping pile of uniform potato slices. It was nice to see my knife skills hadn't deteriorated during my week of self-pity and dark chocolate.

I glanced over at her, and she quickly smoothed out her expression to hide the fact that she was impressed. "Huh." She swept the potatoes into a large pot. "What makes you think the police are monitoring you, exactly?"

"I've seen Detective Drummond's car creeping down the street in front of my building several times. I think he's making sure I haven't skipped town. I don't know why they don't charge me already if that's what they're going to do," I said with a sudden flash of anger.

"Well, I'm sure they don't want to have to backtrack with the press again. So far, they haven't retracted their statement that Roland Patrick killed Amber."

"They haven't?" My jaw fell open. "I just assumed they would have by now. I mean, if they really think I ... did it."

She narrowed her eyes and crossed her arms over her apron-covered chest. "You know, I get a lot of down-on their luck people coming through here."

"I imagine so."

"I don't judge."

"That's probably good," I told her, wondering where this was going.

"Everyone makes mistakes," she said, staring hard at me.

"Oh, for Pete's sake. Are you seriously asking me if I killed Amber?" I didn't know whether to laugh or cry.

"What? No. Don't be a flipping moron. I'm just wondering if it's not *possible* that you did accidentally feed Felix bad fish? I mean, I understand your not wanting to admit it, being a chef and all. But if you just conceded that it could have happened, by mistake, you'll probably get the cops off your back. Pride goeth before the fall and all that." She gave me an encouraging little nod.

I rubbed my forehead and tried to come up with a polite way to tell her she was an idiot without sounding hubristic, if that's even a word. I exhaled slowly. "See, here's the thing, Deb. I *know* I didn't give him food poisoning."

"How can you know for sure? Accidents happen, Rosemary."

I held up my fingers as I ticked off the reasons. "One, the scallops were fresh. I didn't buy them myself, but Alayna used the fishmonger I go to. They looked white and clean, they smelled fresh, and the muscle wasn't pulling away. Two, I prepared them properly. The acid from the limes would have denatured the scallops within fifteen minutes, max. They were safe to eat. Three, I ate them, too. I didn't get sick." *Well, not from the food, at least.*

Her expression grew thoughtful. After a moment she nodded. "Huh, that actually makes sense. And the police know all this?"

I started to say yes but stopped to really think about it. "Um, maybe? Er, no, probably not."

She arched an eyebrow at me. "Maybe you better give tall, dark, and well-mannered a call."

"Pardon?"

She reached into her apron pocket and plucked out a business card. "Detective David Drummond," she read before slipping it back into its spot. "He's stopped by at least three or four time since Amber Patrick died. Seems like he really cares about getting to the bottom of this—and it seems like he cares about you."

~ ~ ~ ~ ~ ~ ~ ~ ~ ~

Detective Drummond squinted at me across the picnic table. "You don't like it," he pronounced.

Actually, I like hot dogs more than any self-respecting holistic chef should admit. But the grilled foot-long was daunting. "No, really, I'm just full. I had a late lunch."

He scrunched his face up skeptically and chewed his dog while he stared at me.

I stared back. "I had a bacon cheeseburger two hours ago, dude. Cut me some slack."

He laughed so hard I thought he was going to choke. "Sorry," he said, taking a swig of his craft beer.

"What's so funny? That I ate a burger?" I could only imagine the false impression this guy had of me.

"Well, yeah, that's funny, too. But I can't believe you just called me 'dude.' I would have expected Detective Dude."

I smiled despite myself. I guess we both had some false impressions to get past. "Fair enough."

He swallowed and leaned forward, placing his elbows on the red-and-white plastic tablecloth. "So what did you want to talk about?"

"Sorry for dragging you out on your day off. It's really not urgent." I fake laughed, feeling self-conscious about bringing up my status as a suspect with a guy about to drip ketchup down the front of his Jimmy Buffett t-shirt.

"Don't do that," he said around a mouthful of bun. "You said you wanted to talk. Talk."

I picked off a piece of the hot dog and nibbled on it. "Um, I was wondering where you guys stood on the investigation. Or, I guess, the investigations—into Amber's death and Felix's ... illness."

"Are you asking if you're still a suspect?" He used his free hand to shield his eyes from the sun so he could get a good look at my face as he asked the question.

"Yes," I answered simply.

"Well, yeah, you are."

I wasn't surprised so much as irritated. "This is so stupid. You *know* somebody was trying to frame me for Amber's murder. I mean, you *know* that."

He polished off his hot dog and raised both hands in a 'don't shoot the messenger' gesture. "Listen, we have a problem. Sullivan still likes Roland Patrick for her murder, but his high-price attorney is making a lot of noise about the fact that you had access to Amber's wine *and* just happened to prepare the meal that nearly killed Felix. He keeps yammering about Occam's razor. Whoever the heck Occam is."

"William of Occam. He was a Franciscan monk who lived in the Middle Ages."

"What's his razor have to do with anything?"

I narrowed my eyes at him. "Is this dumb cop schtick a put on?"

He laughed. "You should say what you're thinking, Rosemary. Don't mince words."

I pursed my lips and waited for him to answer my question.

"Fine," he said finally. "Guilty as charged. Yes, I know what Occam's razor means. And if you do, too, then you know it means things don't look good for you. The simplest explanation is usually the right one."

"What I know is that Pat's lawyer's talking out of his butt, and that's an oversimplification. Occam's razor isn't meant to be used to solve crimes for crying out loud. It's a scientific principle that holds that when there are competing hypotheses of equal predictive ability, you should choose the one that makes the fewest assumptions," I said in a voice I used to reserve for lecturing undermotivated undergraduates when I was a teaching assistant.

He appraised me for a moment. "Oh, that's right. I forgot about your background in chemistry."

The way he said it made a chill run down my spine. I'd assumed the police had looked into my past, but *knowing* that they'd done it, and knowing that he had to know all the ugly details about my parent's financial shenanigans struck me. I felt invaded. And humiliated.

I pushed past my shame and said, "Okay. That's another thing. Given my knowledge of chemistry, I could have easily poisoned both Amber and Felix without leaving a trace."

"Don't repeat that." He leaned forward, all tense and serious. "Do you understand me? You might think that the logic of a statement like that will convince people of your innocence, but it will have the exact opposite effect."

It occurred to me that he probably really shouldn't be coaching me this way; but I was glad he was doing it. "Okay. Got it. I'm just —" I blew my bangs out of my eyes while I tried to put a name to my feeling. "I'm frustrated. I didn't kill Amber. I didn't poison Felix. I can tell you, in as much detail as you need, that those scallops were fresh and properly prepared. Another thing— I ate them, too. I didn't end up in the hospital. The simplest explanation here doesn't involve me at all. But you guys won't listen, and the cloud over my name is ruining my life." It sounded melodramatic, even to me, but it was how I felt.

"Ruining your life," he repeated, leaning back and crossing his arms over his chest. "You mean your love life?"

"Well, yes, as a matter of fact. Felix won't talk to me. So he obviously believes whatever lies you and his dad's lawyers are spinning about me."

"Now hang on. Don't go blaming your romantic troubles on the LAPD. Lover Boy isn't talking to *us*, either."

"He's not?"

"No. He won't cooperate with our investigation. And from what I hear, he won't meet with his father's legal team, either. So, he's not saying anything to help you, but he also isn't saying anything to hurt you—at this point."

This was interesting news, which merited further consideration later. "Okay, well, your stupid investigation is also affecting my career. As in, I'm unemployed and unemployable."

He belly laughed like that was the funniest thing he'd heard all day. Then he wiped actual tears—tears of laughter—from his eyes and caught his breath, "Sorry. That's cute. This is *Hollywood,* Rosemary. It's not like the rest of the world. Your notoriety makes you a hot commodity. Do you mean to tell me your voicemail isn't full of people wanting to interview you, turn your life into a movie of the week, and have you wear their latest fashion design?"

"I haven't listened to my messages, to tell you the truth. I've been too busy." *Yes, very busy hiding in my apartment drowning my sorrows in dark chocolate.*

"Well, let me give you a piece of free advice: you need to strike while the iron's hot. Capitalize on your fame, or infamy, now. Because your fifteen minutes are probably almost up." He crumpled his wrapper into a ball and lobbed it into the nearby trashcan then stood and wiped the crumbs off his pants. It was almost exactly the same advice Deb had given me.

"But if I draw attention to myself like that won't I just piss off Detective Sullivan?"

He shook his head at me like I was a child. "A girl's gotta eat. Sullivan probably thinks it's suspicious that you *aren't* out there giving interviews and hawking your gravy at Whole Foods."

Seventeen

"YOU MEAN, like, people will hire you to cater their events because of the adrenaline rush they'll get from wondering if your cooking will kill them?" Thyme asked.

I could hear Sage breathing heavily and unevenly in a pathetic attempt to hold back her laughter on her end.

"Just go ahead and laugh, Sage. You sound like a pervert," I told her before addressing Thyme's question. "Yeah, it'll be like those people who eat blowfish in Japan."

"Jeez, Rosie, you don't have to be so cranky," Thyme shot back.

"Sorry. But I need to do something to earn some money. And everyone is telling me I should take advantage of my unwanted celebrity." Everyone being one police detective and the woman who runs the kitchen at a homeless shelter, but my sisters didn't need to know the details.

Sage hemmed then said, "Here's the thing. Do you *want* to open a catering business? Because Thyme and I were talking. Despite old Doug the accountant's persistent doom and gloom scenarios, we're making a lot of progress toward cleaning up Mom and Dad's debt. We're in pretty good shape. Good enough shape that we could probably talk to the creditors and get a short extension—maybe an additional twelve months—to pay everything off. So if you wanted to come back here and get back into the lab, well, we'd support that. I mean, if you tell Dave you're moving back home, I'm sure the cops will understand. As long as they can find you, they shouldn't care."

I was too surprised to speak at first. Then I shook my head as if they could see me. "No. Absolutely not. We're getting that monkey off our backs by April, not a moment later. I mean, I appreciate the offer, I *really* do, but no. We're sticking to the plan." I felt my chin jut forward in an expression our father used to call 'Rosemary's obstinate face.'

"You know, you don't have to be a martyr," Sage said.

"I'm not," I insisted.

"We miss you, Rosie," Thyme broke in, speaking in a voice so soft I could barely hear her. "You're so far away out there. And ... all alone."

Tears pricked at my eyes. "I miss you, too. But I'm okay. Honest."

"As okay as someone who's under suspicion for murder and attempted murder can be, you mean?" Sage asked.

"Right." I giggled at the absurdity.

"And Felix just broke up with you," Thyme said, as if I needed to be reminded.

"So?"

"So? So it's our job as your sisters to take you out dancing and shopping and stuff to take your mind off it," Thyme told me.

"Oh, please. We only dated for, what, a month? And we never even ... you know. I don't need to get over Felix. I'm already over him," I lied as convincingly as I could.

"Right, of course you are. There's nothing remotely traumatic about being barfed on and then dumped," Sage deadpanned.

"Almost barfed on," I corrected her, setting off a fresh round of laughter.

Between howls of laughter, Thyme observed, "You forgot arrested and fired."

After we could all breathe again, we said our good-byes. I hated to cut short a call with my sisters, but I had a to-do list as long as my arm if I was going to get Rosemary's Gravy, A Special Occasion Catering Service, up and running. I may have been lying about being okay with what happened with Felix, but I wasn't lying at all when I said I wasn't being a martyr. Somehow, cooking for other people had become something I enjoyed, not something I had to do out of financial necessity. It had happened without my even noticing it. I was looking forward to starting a catering business, even if it did involve a ton of work—starting with about a million preliminary tasks.

And, unfortunately, one of the first tasks on the list was to make an unannounced appearance at the Patrick residence.

~ ~ ~ ~ ~ ~ ~ ~ ~ ~

I stood for a long time on the lawn in front of the Patricks' mansion before I forced myself to ascend the wide staircase and pass under the shadow of the utterly unnecessary and sort of pretentious columns flanking the door. I smoothed my hair and skirt and took a deep breath and exhaled. Then I jabbed the doorbell and listened to my heart knock around in my chest while I pretended to hope that Alayna answered the door even though I happened to know that she usually ran to the post office on Tuesday afternoons to check Pat's P.O. Box.

A minute or so passed, and I was just about to ring the bell again, when the door opened and I came face to face with Felix for the first time since the night I'd held his hand in the back of an ambulance.

He took a half step backward, almost as if he actually believed I *had* poisoned him and had shown up to finish the job. My hammering heart skipped a beat.

"Um, hi," I managed.

He nodded but continued to eyeball me warily.

When he didn't say anything, I pressed on. "I'm sorry to bother you but I need to get my recipes off the kitchen iPad. I need them for my new job." I smiled impersonally.

"Oh. Really? My dad didn't mention anyone calling to check your references," he said in a stiff, weird-sounding voice.

Spoken like a true trust fund kid—as if I would ask Roland Patrick for a reference. I couldn't begin to imagine what he'd say about me. Even though Felix hadn't invited me in, he also hadn't slammed the door in my face, so I took three quick steps and propelled myself into the entry foyer before he could shut me out. Then I said, "I'm starting my own company, but I really need those recipes."

"Oh, right. Sure." He just stood there, staring at me.

An involuntary image of his hands roaming over my body while his lips pressed hungrily on my neck flashed through my mind and I felt my legs start to tremble. I leaned against the wall in a faux casual pose and said, "So what you said before—that Pat didn't mention me—does that mean you and your dad are on speaking terms?"

He wet his lips, and I got the feeling he had a similar image running through his head. "Yeah, we are. He's still staying at Antonio's. We're working things out, though. In our own way."

"That's great," I said with a sincerity I truly felt.

"Yeah." He swallowed hard. "I guess that was one good thing about your quitting; it got us talking again."

"My ... quitting?" I blinked at him and tilted my head, sure I'd misheard him.

He blinked back at me. "Right."

I let my breath out in a long whoosh. "Wow. Okay, I didn't quit. Your dad fired me."

"He fired you?"

"Yeah. His lawyer sent me a letter." Leave it to Pat to spin it like I quit. I narrowed my eyes, "Wait. Did you leave instructions at the hospital that you didn't want to speak to me?" I asked. If the answer was 'yes,' it was going to sting, but knowing that Pat had lied about firing me, I had to wonder if he'd also been behind the brick wall that had sprung up between me and Felix.

His face turned white then red then finally purple with rage. "What? That's ... I never freaking said that. My dad told me you left town. I figured you moved back East without even saying goodbye."

My head was swimming. All this time, I'd been thinking he'd shut me out, and he'd been sitting here believing I'd abandoned him?

I shook my head. "No," I said in a soft voice, "I've been worried about you."

His eyes darkened with a desire I recognized and he drew closer to me. "I've missed you," he said. His mouth was so close to mine that our breath mingled when he spoke.

I could feel myself getting ready to melt into a puddle of sexual tension but some part of my brain was screaming at me to keep my wits about me. That still-functioning gray matter reminded me that nothing had stopped him from driving by my apartment or picking up the phone to confirm what Pat had said. I just needed to get copies of my recipes and get out of there.

It took all of my resolve, but I squared my shoulders and coughed. "The recipes?"

His eyes registered hurt and his face took on a closed expression as he stepped away from me. "Oh, right. Sure. You know where the iPad is. Take what you need. I was just heading to the studio. Just ... let yourself out and set the alarm when you're done, okay?" His voice was cool.

"Okay, thanks," I mumbled. I stared down at my sandals for a moment and noted that my toenail polish was chipping. I raised my head and said to his departing back. "Wait."

He turned and gave me an expectant smile. "Yeah?"

"I want to make sure you know this: you didn't get food poisoning from my ceviche."

His smile faded. "I don't care, either way, Rosemary. Accidents happen. I just thought we had something real. Guess I was wrong."

"So did I," I answered in an even voice. "But you sure didn't make any effort to get ahold of me when you got out of the hospital. I at least tried to reach you."

He set his mouth in a hard line. "You know what? To hell with this. There are plenty of girls who'd love to be with me. You really don't know your place." Then he turned on his heel and walked through the door, slamming it behind him like a petulant teenager.

My place? My place? I wandered into the kitchen on autopilot, trembling with anger. I sent up a quick prayer of gratitude to the universe that I had insisted on all those proper dates before we got intimate. Bullet narrowly dodged there.

I heard his car engine spring to life. He peeled out of the garage before I'd even powered on the iPad and found my file of recipes. My fingers were shaking as I opened up the staff browser and copied the file to Drop-box. I had copies of most of my recipes or had them memorized, but cooking for Amber had involved a lot of parties. The modifications I'd made to feed large crowds were work I'd otherwise have to recreate. So despite the bruising to my ego and the fact that I could already tell there would be a milkshake consumed through a stream of mortified tears in my future, I was glad I'd come. To my own amazement, I realized I was more excited about building my business than I was distraught about the fact that Felix had turned out to be a dick.

All the same, I'd be glad to get out here as soon as possible. I tapped my foot against the tile and waited for the files to upload. Once I was sure I had them all safely floating in the Cloud or wherever they were, I was about to power down the device when I had a sudden thought. Alayna's files contained a list of vendors that Amber had used for events—places where she rented extra glass-ware, linens, tents, outdoor heaters, whatever. I might as well save myself some time and use services that I knew had met with Amber's approval. I opened Alayna's folder to copy the spreadsheet, certain that she wouldn't mind.

As I scrolled through her files, an email notification from Amazon popped up in the corner of the screen. "Amber Patrick, how many stars would you give *'Botu-linum Toxin Applications in Medicine: Miracle Poison'?* The subject line barely registered at first, but after a few seconds, my fingers stopped moving and my brain started working.

When had I *ever* seen Amber reading a book? Answer: never. She *could* read, I knew, as she read scripts, reviews about her performances, and gossip columns. But a medical textbook? Not a chance. My finger moved to the email pop up and hovered over the screen for several, seemingly interminable seconds. I knew that I was about to snoop. And I felt moderately bad about it.

But I couldn't just ignore the warning signals my brain was sending. Botulinum toxin is serious stuff. Produced by the bacterium *Clostridium botulinum,* the toxin is highly poisonous *and* just happens to cause botulism, a type of food poisoning that resulted in vomiting, paralysis, and sometimes death.

I made up my mind and clicked the email notification, holding my breath as I scanned it. Someone—not Amber, unless her Prime membership extended into the afterworld—had used Amber's account to order the textbook just four days before my ill-fated romantic evening with Felix. The one that was interrupted by a bout of vomiting, paralysis, but, thankfully, not death.

I stared at the email, heart thumping, and tried to process what I'd read. The only person who'd been living at the house when the book was delivered was Felix. But surely, he wouldn't have poisoned *himself* with something so deadly in an effort to set me up. Nobody was *that* crazy.

And, leaving aside the insanity of such a thing, how would he have gotten his hands on the toxin itself. I knew from my time working in university labs that highly poisonous substances are tightly controlled. Sure, you might be able to order them online with the click of a mouse, but they were only shipped to accredited research institutions with prior authorization to order them. No, there was no way Felix had poisoned himself.

But the book ...

The garage door slammed. I jumped and then powered off the iPad and shoved it back into its holder. I was digging out my keys and slinking toward the front of the house to avoid another round with Felix when the garage door opened.

I let out an enormous sigh of relief at the sight of Alayna, her arms laden with carefully packaged demo CDs sent by aspiring musicians. One night this week, Pat would get a good laugh out of mocking some kids' dreams over a bottomless gin rickey. It seemed to be one his favorite pastimes.

Alayna dumped the packages on the counter and narrowed her eyes as me. "I thought that was your car in the driveway."

"Hello to you, too," I said. I was sort of put off by her prickliness but then it occurred to me that Pat had probably lied to her, too. "I didn't quit, you know. Pat fired me."

"Hmph. Is that so?" she said, her tone softening slightly.

"Yes."

"Then what are you doing here?" Her gaze shifted to the ceiling. "Are you waiting for Felix? His car's not in the garage."

The mention of Felix made me tense all over again, just when I'd started to relax. Alayna and I have never openly discussed the fact that Felix and I had been dating. But it hadn't taken a rocket scientist to pick up on the hormones that had been flying around the house. And Alayna was no dummy. She was the second ranked student in her night division program and had mentioned she was thinking about applying to medical school.

Medical school. The textbook. I nearly slapped my forehead like a character on a sit-com, but I managed to restrain myself. "No, no. I just needed to get copies of my recipes off the iPad. Felix let me in, but had to go somewhere. I'm all done. So, I'll just let myself out." I smiled and booked out of there before she had a chance to stop me.

I flat out ran to the Saab. I turned the key to start the ignition with shaky hands and sped down the canyon road as quickly as I dared. I wanted to be far away when Alayna realized I'd seen the email about the botulinum toxin book.

Eighteen

I DROVE STRAIGHT TO THE police station and asked the desk sergeant to let Detective Drummond know I was in the lobby and urgently needed to talk to him.

She shifted her gaze from the computer monitor and paused her fingers over the keyboard. She gave me an amused look and blew her short bangs off her forehead. "Honey, he ain't up there."

"Where is he?"

"Out protecting and serving, ma'am."

Oh. Right. Well, crap, now what? I considered my only other option, which was unpalatable to put it mildly.

She watched me impassively for a few seconds while I debated myself silently before she got bored and turned back to her computer monitor.

I sighed. "Is Detective Sullivan available?"

That got her attention. She peered at me over the counter. "You're asking to see *her?*" she asked as if she must have misheard me.

"I guess so. Unless you can reach Detective Drummond somehow? It's really important."

"I can give you his mobile number."

"I have it, but I need to speak to him in person."

She pursed her lips.

"It's about one of his cases," I continued in an effort to convince her.

Her right eyebrow shot up to her hairline. "I figured that much. I recognize you, you know. You're the killer chef."

"I beg your pardon?"

"Oh, sorry. That's what they're calling you on the Morning Show with Mort and Moxie."

"They're talking about me on the radio?"

"They're talking about you everywhere."

I blushed a deep red. I didn't think I'd ever get used to being a quasi-public figure. Then I took a deep breath and decided there was no time like the present to practice my marketing skills. "They'll really be talking once my catering business is up and running."

"No, you're not!"

"I am," I assured her. "Rosemary's Gravy, A Special Occasion Catering Service, will provide a mouth-watering, memorable meal for special events ranging from an intimate party to a gala affair."

She nodded like she was semi-impressed. "Not bad. That name's a mouthful, though."

"You think?"

"I'd keep it short and sweet. Just go with Rosemary's Gravy."

"Hmm. Thanks." I'd have to give that some thought. "So, Detective Drummond?"

"Yeah, he's not really out on patrol or anything."

"He's not?" Now I was just confused.

She scribbled an address onto a scrap of paper and handed it to me. "Don't tell him who told you where to find him."

I shoved the paper into my purse and flashed her a smile. "My lips are sealed. Thanks."

"No problem. Hey, do you have a card?"

Business cards. I made a mental note to add that to the list. "Um, they're not back from the printer yet." Which was totally true. I hadn't sent them to the printer, so they clearly weren't back yet.

"Drop one off when you get them. My aunt and uncle are celebrating their fiftieth wedding anniversary next month. They'd get a kick out of having the killer chef cater it."

I floated out of the police station too excited to be offended. For about half a minute I almost forgot why I'd gone there. But it came rushing back fast enough.

~ ~ ~ ~ ~ ~ ~ ~ ~ ~

I was about eight miles away from the address the desk sergeant had given me when I decided either my phone was hopelessly confused or the woman had pranked me for her own amusement. The congestion of the city had given way to a desolate, rural landscape. Parched brown grass, chain link fences, and abandoned lots lined the highway. I passed a closed gas station and the burned out shell of a strip club. I told myself that if the scenery didn't improve and fast, I'd pull over and call Detective Drummond's cell phone, which I should have just done in the first place.

After another stretch of emptiness, a crematorium appeared on the horizon as I crested a hill.

"That's it," I said aloud.

I turned off the highway and parked in the entrance of the trailer park to fumble through my purse for Detective Drummond's card, wishing I'd put his number in my contacts file the first time I'd had to call him. But, at the time, it had seemed weird to have a police detective in my contacts. You know what they say about hind-sight.

I found the card and was keying in the numbers when a sharp rap on my driver's window made me jump. I looked up to see a wizened man with leathery skin sitting erect in a golf cart, his bald head glistening in the mid-day heat, peering in at me.

I pressed the button to lower the window, hoping I wasn't about to be mugged by a senior citizen. "Uh, hi. I'm sorry, am I blocking the exit? I'll be out of here in a second." I held up the phone as if to show him I just had to make a call.

"Nah, I'm not going anywhere. This thing's not street legal. Though she should be—I can get 'er up to forty-five miles an hour." He patted the front of the cart in a proud, satisfied gesture.

"Really? I had no idea a golf cart could go that fast."

He nodded wisely. "Made some modifications. Anyhow, I figure you're lost. Wanted to see if you need directions."

"Oh. Um, actually, I am and I do."

"Thought as much. We don't get many visitors out here. And I know most everybody's families and whatnot. Didn't recognize your car. Now most folks who come up this way and get turned around are headed to Blush. Is that where you're going?"

I looked at him blankly. "I don't know. Let me check the address."

As I reached for it, he added, "It's a nudist colony, Blush." He winked.

A nudist colony? My face flushed. I dearly hoped that my destination wasn't Blush. I rattled off the address the desk sergeant had given me and held my breath.

He shook his head, a little sadly, I thought. "No, that's not Blush. The Blush people bought the land back behind the crematorium but it's hard to see the entrance. You've already passed it. You're in good shape. Go up the road a piece, and in about three minutes you'll see a parking lot on the left side of the road. Turn in there." He turned the key in his ignition and started to swing his cart back around toward the interior of the trailer park without waiting for a thank you.

I leaned my head out the window and called after him, "Sir, wait! The address—if it's not Blush, what is it?"

He raised a hand and waved goodbye but either didn't hear my question or didn't care to drive back to answer it. Well, as long as everyone there would be fully dressed, I supposed it didn't much matter what it was. I backed the car out of the trailer park and merged into the light traffic flowing toward north.

~ ~ ~ ~ ~ ~ ~ ~ ~ ~

It definitely wasn't a nudist colony. It was an animal shelter. I could hear the cacophony of barking dogs before I even pulled into the lot. The noise and the sign—Rescue Haven—relieved my concerns about what I might be walking into. I parked in a hurry, maybe a little crooked but didn't bother to straighten it out. I hopped out of the car and jogged up to the front doors of the building. A group of dogs playing in the fenced-in area behind the structure raced over to the fence to bark and jump at me in greeting.

I pushed the door open and headed for the reception area. A fat, striped tomcat sunning himself in the exact middle of the counter opened one eye to appraise me. Apparently unimpressed, he closed it again. A wiry guy with olive skin and spiky hair smiled at me. "Hi, there. Don't mind Bongo. He thinks he's in charge around here."

"I see that," I answered returning his smile.

"Can I help you?"

"I hope so. I'm looking for Detect ... Dave Drummond."

He nodded. "You're in the right place. He's back there in the kennel." He jerked a thumb toward the hallway to his right. "Can you find it? I'm the only one in the front today, and, despite my best efforts, I haven't been able to convince Bongo to answer the phones."

"I'm sure I can manage."

He nodded his thanks. Bongo snored blissfully.

I pushed through the swinging door and walked along a short corridor that opened into a large, square room with block walls, a cement floor, and approximately seven million dogs if the noise level was a guide. Just like their outdoor brethren had, as soon as they saw me, the canines rushed to the front of their kennels to greet me with varying degrees of enthusiasm, ferocity, and curiosity, tails wagging and noses wriggling. I spotted Detective Drummond near the back of the room.

My heart melted. He was crouched down, his hand outstretched, trying to coax a shivering mutt from the far corner of a cage. Then, he turned to see what the ruckus was about and met my eyes. His look of concern reminded me why I'd trekked out there, and my gooey emotion was replaced by a new dose of anxiety. He was about to stand up when the pup behind him nudged its nose forward and into his hand.

"Don't move," I called. I walked toward him slowly, hoping I wouldn't spook the poor animal.

He nodded and returned his attention to the dog. By the time I reached them, he had a hand around the creature's middle and was scratching its torn ear.

"I'm assuming Sergeant Bentley told you where to find me," he said by way of greeting, keeping his voice low and gentle.

"She did." I bent and offered the back of my palm to the dog.

As it sniffed my hand, Detective Drummond continued, "And I'm assuming you're not here because you want to adopt a pet."

"Right. Well, I'd love to get a cat, actually, but my lease says no pets."

"Mine, too. And the hours I work aren't really conducive to pet ownership. So I come out here once a week and walk the dogs, help out with the food." The dog rolled over to show her belly—it was a she, and it looked as though she'd been nursing pups until quite recently. He scratched her belly. "Good girl, Mona Lisa."

"What's her story?"

"Someone was using her to breed hunting dogs. The creep abandoned her when she outlived her useful purpose, I guess. We named her Mona Lisa because sometimes she looks like she's smiling, but there's something forlorn about her smile. You didn't answer my question, Rosemary." He stood up and grabbed a harness and leash hanging from a peg on the wall and looped it around the dog.

I was so caught up in Mona Lisa's sad history that I almost forgot why I was there. I blurted, "I know who killed Amber!"

His expression was entirely unreadable. He was silent for a moment then said, "Let's walk. It's noisy in here, and Mona Lisa loves to be outside."

I followed him through a metal door that led out to the fenced-in yard. Mona Lisa shied away from the other dogs in the pen, and Detective Drummond hustled her through the chaos and out a gate set in the chain link fence. We followed a gravel path through some scraggly trees and into an overgrown lot. Neither of us spoke until the shelter was out of sight. Then he said, "Spill it."

I looked down at Mona Lisa, who was now prancing around on the end of the leash, sniffing every blade of grass and patch of weeds like the world's happiest dog. I inhaled, filling my abdomen and lungs with air the way Thyme was always nagging me to breathe, and then exhaled slowly while I gathered my thoughts. "It was Alayna," I began.

He spoke before I could go on. "Ramirez? The housekeeper?"

"Right."

"How sure are you?"

I was about to insist I was positive, when I stopped to think. "Well, I'm assuming she did it."

"You're *assuming* she killed Amber Patrick? You came all the way out here to waste my time with your *assumptions?*" He shot me a disgusted look and shook his head. "Come on, Mona Lisa," he said, tugging on her leash and turning to leave.

"Wait." I put my hand on his bare forearm to stop him. He stared at my hand but made no effort to shake it off, so I kept talking. "I assume she killed Amber because I know she poisoned Felix. I had to go to the house today to get some of my things." I hesitated at the memory of my run-in with Felix.

"I bet that was awkward. Was lover boy there?"

I removed my hand from his warm skin and narrowed my eyes, unsure of whether he was mocking me or genuinely being sympathetic in a stoic guy sort of way. He looked back at me impassively, so I decided to give him the benefit of the doubt. "He was there, but he left and told me to let myself out when I was done."

Mona Lisa pulled on her leash, urging Detective Drummond forward. "Let's keep walking," he said. "This path leads back to a creek. It's not much to look at, but Mona Lisa likes to splash around in it."

"Okay."

We walked a few paces and then he said, "What did you have to get out of there anyway? It's not like you had a desk or locker to clean out."

"I took your advice to capitalize on my misfortune. I'm starting a catering business."

You know how people will say someone's smile lit up his face? Well, I've never seen it actually happen before, but in this case, it did. He grinned broadly at the news and his entire face softened.

"That's fantastic!"

I smiled back at him. "Thanks. I'm pretty excited. But I needed some of my recipes that I used for big parties, so I copied them off the iPad in the kitchen." A sudden worry twisted its way into my stomach. "Oh, no, that's okay, right? It won't mess up your investigation?"

He waved my concern away. "Nah, don't sweat it. The computer geeks imaged the drive or whatever it is they do. They have an exact copy of it as it existed when Amber died. And I think they're still monitoring it for changes, as a matter of fact."

That was a relief on two counts. One, I hadn't screwed up any evidence, and, two, even if Alayna had deleted the email while I was driving all over Los Angeles County, the authorities would still have a record of it. "Oh, okay. Good. So, I was uploading the things I needed to the Cloud when an email came in on Amber's account —"

"Amber's email is still active?"

I shrugged. "Apparently. I guess Pat's had other things on his mind and hasn't deactivated it yet. Anyway, it was an email asking her to review a book about botulinum toxin." I finished the sentence with so much drama in my voice that the dog twisted around and whined as if I'd piqued her curiosity. For his part, Detective Drummond stared blankly at me.

"One more time—in English."

"Someone bought a book about botulism using Amber's account *after* she died. It had to have been Alayna; she used Amber's Amazon account to buy stuff for the house all the time. No one else had access."

"Botulism?"

I'm sure you've heard of it; it's a form of food poisoning."

"You get it from eating stuff from bulging cans?" he ventured.

"Right, among other things. It can be deadly and symptoms include vomiting, disorientation, and—wait for it—paralysis. Sound familiar?"

Mona Lisa pawed at a butterfly while Detective Drummond processed this information. "So you're saying Felix was suffering from botulism?"

"Bingo. But it wasn't from my meal—as I've been saying. For one thing, he had to have been exposed several hours, maybe even a day, before he ate the ceviche. You know that food poisoning isn't instantaneous."

"That's what the lab folks said. That the timing was off. But we can't really work up a timeline because Felix isn't interested in cooperating with the investigation."

"Well, maybe he'll be interested in knowing that, for some inexplicable reason, Alayna tried to kill him."

Detective Drummond dropped his gaze to the ground and chewed on his lower lip for several seconds, then he cleared his throat. "It's not exactly inexplicable."

"It's not?"

He looped Mona Lisa's leash around his wrist and touched my shoulder with his free hand. "I'm sorry to be the one to tell you this, but when we were investigating

Amber's death, we pulled the cell phone records for everyone in the house. Alayna and Felix ... well, I guess you'd call what they were doing ... sexting." He gave my shoulder cap a gentle squeeze and then removed his hand.

I wrinkled my forehead in confusion. "They're involved?"

"They were. The texts stopped a few days before Amber's murder."

We stared at each other. I don't know what he was thinking about. I was thinking about the simmering hostility between Alayna and Felix that had run through the house like an undercurrent. Finally I said, "Alayna killed her." I wasn't sure exactly why. But it would have been beyond easy for her to slip a little peanut oil into a wine bottle.

"It's possible, but she has no motive—at least, no better motive than anyone else who's been on the receiving end of Amber's crap stick," he said. His brown eyes were serious and had a faraway look.

"I think she knows I know. Or she will soon. She'll be able to tell I read the email."

"Great." I could tell he wanted to shake me for being so careless, but we both knew I couldn't undo it. To his credit, he didn't bother to scold me.

"So now what?"

"Now we finish Mona Lisa's walk. Then I'm going to need your help."

Nineteen

I'M NOT SURE WHAT I thought my role would be after I told Detective Drummond what I knew. But I definitely did *not* think I'd find myself back at the police station. This time, though, instead of giving me marketing tips, the desk sergeant was fitting me for a bulletproof vest.

"Why exactly do I need this?" I asked Sergeant Bentley as she cinched the straps snugly and stepped back to critique her work.

"Once you put your shirt back on, no one will even know you're wearing it. The technology sure has improved," she said more to herself than to me.

It was true that the vest was surprisingly sleek and light. But I wasn't about to be distracted from my somewhat crucial question. "Sure, okay. But why is it necessary?"

"It's department policy that civilian participants in all operations be fully protected. It's probably overkill, honestly. Uh, sorry, poor word choice. Look, it's just a precaution. We'd rather suit you up needlessly than defend a lawsuit down the road brought by your grieving relatives. Okay?"

Not really. "Um, I guess."

She smiled encouragingly. "Detective Drummond's running through the plan with Detective Sullivan. They'll be in shortly. Go ahead and get dressed," As she left the room, she patted my upper arm in a reassuring gesture.

I stared after her when the door closed in some sort of shocked disbelief that I was actually standing in the middle of the police station wearing Kevlar. Did they expect me to go see Alayna and get her to confess? Not. A. Chance. I pulled my shirt on over the vest and smoothed it down. Luckily, the blouse was one of those peasanty, billowy things that floated away from my body. Sergeant Bentley was right—no one would be able to tell I was wearing the vest.

I distracted myself from my swirling anxiety about what might come next by pacing in a tight circle in the center of the room until I heard rapid footsteps approaching.

Someone rapped on the door then pushed it open without pausing a beat. Detective Sullivan rushed into the room, and Detective Drummond followed a step behind, trotting in an effort to keep up with her.

The senior detective strode toward me with a wide politician's smile plastered on her face and extended her hand. "Ms. Field, I misjudged you. Thank you for agreeing to help us catch a killer. It's good to know you consider it your civic duty to assist us." She caught my hand in her steel grip and pumped it vigorously. I suddenly wished I were wearing protective mittens in addition to the vest.

I still wasn't sure what I'd signed up to do, but the dragon lady's enthusiasm for the undertaking convinced me it would be dangerous and ill-advised. I threw Detective Drummond a desperate, panicked glance over her head and massaged the bones in my right hand.

He nodded as if he understood my worry and said, "You'll be in absolutely no danger at any time." He'd slipped back into his serious policeman voice again. The transformation was so complete that I almost couldn't believe this was the same man who'd allowed Mona Lisa to bathe his face in dog slobber when she "kissed" him goodbye before we left the shelter.

"That's good to hear, but I'd feel a lot better about this whole thing if I knew exactly what you expect me to do," I told them neutrally.

"Of course," Detective Sullivan agreed with another big smile. I couldn't believe I actually liked her better as bad cop. But I guess that role played to her strengths; this good cop schtick didn't suit her at all. She cut her eyes toward Detective Drummond and nodded.

He took a step closer and said, "Here's the situation. We can't expect the Patricks to cooperate with us on this. At this point, the relationship between the family and the department is fairly strained. We've been instructed not to contact them directly—only through the family's lawyers." He screwed up his face into an expression that left little doubt how he felt about that development.

"And you want me to go see Alayna and get her to confess?" I fidgeted. On the one hand, she hadn't tried to kill *me*. Yet. On the other, she didn't seem to have any qualms about trying to pin her crimes on me, so I had to figure I wasn't on her list of BFFs.

"No, of course not," he said firmly. "That would be foolish and dangerous. We just need you to talk to Felix and get him to agree to let us into the mansion to take a look around. Detective Sullivan doesn't want to request a search warrant just yet. Those requests have a habit of getting leaked to the press."

Oh, just talk to Felix, that's all. My tapping foot picked up the tempo and I forced myself to be still. "I think I'd rather face Alayna." I flashed him a grim smile to let him know I was kidding.

"I know things ended badly between the two of you. I'd suggest talking to Pat instead ..." He trailed off and let me imagine trying to convince Pat to do anything. Unless they outfitted me with a firehose full of gin, I probably had a better shot with Felix.

"I'd say my relationship with the family is, um, pretty strained, too. Pat fired me, and Felix broke up with me."

"He'll agree to see you, and you know it," Detective Drummond encouraged me. "Just call him up and use that sexy voice of yours."

Detective Sullivan's eyes widened in surprise. I knew the feeling. *Sexy voice?* I stared at Detective Drummond for a long moment. His face turned light pink and he coughed into his fist.

"I'll give it a try, I guess." After Detective Drummond's little bombshell that Felix and Alayna had had a thing, I had zero desire to see Felix ever again. But thinking of Alayna steeled me. No way was I going to let her get away with murder and attempted murder—especially because she kept trying to pin her crimes on yours truly.

A genuine smile creased Detective Drummond's face and spread all the way to his eyes. "Thank you."

I called Felix's cell phone number while Detective Sullivan leaned forward and stared at me with the intensity of a hawk getting ready to take down a rabbit. Between rings, I listened to my heart hammering in my chest, every beat straining against the tight bulletproof vest.

"Rosemary?" Felix answered with mild surprise in his voice.

"Yeah, hi. I ... I need to talk to you," I blurted, cursing the police for not giving me a word-for-word script.

"Oh. I'm getting ready to head over to the apartment to pick up some music one of the artists left there by mistake. Why don't you meet me there?"

I wheeled around and met Detective Sullivan's eyes. Going to the apartment hadn't been part of the plan. In a perfect world, I'd have convinced him over the phone, but the cops had been prepared to drive me over to the mansion. I asked the question with my eyebrows.

She raised a finger to her lip like I might forget that I had Felix on the speakerphone. Then she shifted her eyes sideways to Detective Drummond, who shrugged as if to say 'why not?' She looked back at me and nodded once. A brisk, curt nod.

"Okay, sure," I managed weakly.

"I'll see you there in twenty?"

"Great."

"I'll stop at the taquaria and pick up some food. We can sit out in the garden and have a late dinner under the stars." His voice was husky and inviting—a big shift from his pissy attitude when I'd seen him at the house. I knew he was thinking I'd changed my mind about us.

"No! I mean, no thanks, I already ate."

"See you in a bit."

I pressed the button to end the call with shaking fingers and turned to Detective Drummond. "Let's get this over with already."

Twenty

WE DROVE THE SHORT DISTANCE to the apartment in silence. Detective Drummond drove, and Detective Sullivan sat in the back seat and tapped out furious emails on her phone. I stared out the window at the neighborhood that had become so familiar to me in such a short time. The taco joint, the car wash, the concrete playground covered in graffiti flashed past my eyes. Although the usual stop-and-go traffic was in effect, Detective Drummond slapped a light up on the top of the unmarked car, and we zipped through the congestion.

He pulled into the driveway on the side of the apartment building, bringing the car to a rest right behind

Felix's Boxter. He twisted in his seat to study my face. "You ready?"

I nodded.

"Piece of cake, remember? Tell him as much or as little as you think you need to get him to agree. When he gives the go-ahead, come to the door and signal us to come in. We'll get verbal confirmation from him and then send a unit to take you back to your car. Okay?"

"Okay. But I can walk back to the station to pick up my car." The last thing I wanted to do was hang around the apartment with Felix waiting for a ride.

"Negative," Detective Sullivan interrupted without even glancing up from her phone. "The department is going to ensure your safety until the end of this thing. You're not going to wander through gang territory, not even wearing a vest. You'll get a ride back with a uniform." Her voice brooked no argument.

"Fine, whatever." I just wanted this to be over already. I reached for the door handle.

"Rosemary—" Detective Drummond said.

I paused. "What?"

"Good luck."

A look passed between us. I got that feeling that he had a lot to say, but he couldn't say any of it in front of his boss. For my part, adrenaline was racing through my body making it difficult to think clearly. So I shot him a smile and opened the door.

I walked slowly along the path to the front of the building, highly conscious of the fact that they were watching me from inside the vehicle. With each heavy step, I wanted to turn back. I saw myself tearing off the vest and running all the way back to my car at the police station. Driving to the airport and getting the first flight back east, leaving the insanity of Los Angeles behind. Fleeing all of life's complications.

An image of my parents sailing off in clear blue waters, away from their responsibilities, popped into my mind.

No. I can do this. I will do this.

I set my mouth in a firm line and forced myself to keep walking toward the door. I tried to ignore the acid roiling in my stomach and focused instead on the jasmine-scented breeze. I took two deep breaths and then reached out to ring the bell, but Felix pulled the door open before I pressed the button.

"Hi," he said simply, smiling his brilliant white smile. His hair was damp, as if he'd just showered, and curling slightly over his forehead. His cream-colored button-down shirt set off both his tan and his green eyes. He wore faded jeans. His feet were bare.

I stared at him for a few seconds, wondering if he had somehow managed to become even more attractive since I'd seen him that morning. He looked back at me in mild amusement, as if he could read my mind. I shook myself out of my daze.

"Um, hi. Can I come in?"

"I guess. Nice ride," he commented as he stepped aside and focused on the Crown Victoria in his driveway.

I paused on the threshold and gave Detective Drummond and Detective Sullivan a little wave. "It's a long story," I said before continuing into the apartment on unsteady legs.

He lingered in the doorway, peering at the car with narrowed eyes, then shut the door firmly. He turned to face me. "Is this a social visit or police business, Rosemary?" His expression was closed and hard, and I recognized the tight, strained voice of a person who thought he'd been played for a fool.

I reminded myself that even rich people have feelings. "A little of both," I admitted. "Can we sit down?"

He didn't answer but crossed the hallway into the sitting room and took a seat one of the club chairs, so I took that as a yes. I followed him and lowered myself into the chair across from him, waiting for him to speak. He sat stiffly, spine rigid, head erect. I did, too, mainly because it turns out it's not possible to slouch while wearing a protective vest.

Finally, his shoulders relaxed and his face opened. "So are you going to tell me what this about? Because it's clearly not about us."

Us. The thought of there being an us ripped through me with an almost-physical pain. I pushed it away and focused on the reason I was here.

"Sure. Detective Sullivan and Detective Drummond are in the car. They want your permission to look around the mansion."

He exploded out of his chair, waving his arms wildly. "Are you freaking serious? You came here to wheedle me into letting them search the house for more evidence against my dad? What's wrong with you?" he raged, red-faced.

This wasn't going well. I hurried to my feet. "It's not like that, Felix," I implored him. "Listen to me." I reached out a tentative hand to still his arm. At my touch, he stopped flailing and pinned me with a distrustful look.

"What's it like, then?"

"Alayna killed Amber. I don't know why, but I'm sure she did." He let out a snort. I couldn't tell if the sound meant laughter, disbelief, or more anger, so I rushed on, "And I know she tried to poison you ... that night." Being in the apartment with him again was throwing me even more off-balance than I'd anticipated, and my voice hitched.

"That night," he repeated hoarsely.

I swallowed around the lump in my throat. "That night. When you got so sick, it wasn't from the scallops. Somehow, Alayna managed to expose you to a toxin called botulinum," I said, forcing myself to think about the poison and not the hungry way he'd looked at me before the toxin had taken effect.

My words seemed to stop his mounting desire in its tracks. His eyes, which had become heavy-lidded and soft, snapped open. "Botulinum? Like Botox?" he asked.

The undercurrent of urgency was unmistakable. "Well, yeah, sort of. It's produced by the same bacterium that's used cosmetically, but it can be fatal when it's ingested."

My knowledge about the use of the toxin as a cosmetic treatment was very limited. A few years earlier, my parents had been approached by a dermatology outfit about adding its services to the spa's menu. My dad had asked me, as the family scientist, if it was truly safe. I'd told him that as far as I knew, it was, but he'd decided that injecting poison into a person's wrinkles didn't really fit with the spa's natural mission anyway.

"Botox," Felix repeated. He bounced on the balls of his bare feet.

"What am I missing?"

"Amber had regular Botox treatments."

"Why? She didn't have a single line on her face."

He shrugged. "We're talking about Hollywood, Rosemary. She was terrified of aging out of the hot girlfriend role and into the mom role."

I could feel myself winding up for a rant about the ageism and sexism in the movie industry, but I squelched it and settled for giving him a look of sheer disbelief. I had more important topics to discuss. "Okay, so Amber saw a dermatologist. That's sort of irrelevant to the fact that Alayna got her hands on botulinum toxin. Isn't it?"

"No. I don't think it is. As terrified as Amber was of getting old, she was equally terrified of being perceived as someone who was worried about aging. Follow?"

"Not really. But keep going."

"She was really concerned that some nurse or receptionist or someone would leak the story that she used Botox to the tabloids. So she got my dad to find her some doctor in Mexico who would sell the stuff to inject into herself at home."

I'd seen a lot of crazy things working for Amber Patrick, but the idea that she was buying back alley Botox from Mexico kind of took the cake. "Are you being serious?"

"Oh, yeah. But there's more. It's not like Amber was going to handle that transaction in person."

"She sent Pat?"

It was his turn to give me the 'you can't be serious' look. "Oh, hell, no. She sent Alayna."

Of course she did. Sending her Hispanic maid over the border to do her dirty work was a move straight out of Amber's playbook. "No wonder Alayna killed her," I said more to myself than to him.

He shook his head and took a deep breath. He exhaled slowly then looked me straight in the eye and said, "That's not why Alayna killed her—if she killed her." He paused and cleared his throat. "A few days before Amber died, she found out Alayna and I were dating and threatened to fire her."

Time seemed to slow down, way down, and his voice sounded distorted and garbled in my ears. "You were *dating* Alayna?" When Detective Drummond mentioned sexting, I figured the two of them had carried on a mild flirtation. That was one thing. But dating ...

"For a while. It was nothing serious, Rosemary. Not like what we—"

I raised my palm. "Don't. Please. When was this?"

He winced before answering. "I broke up with her the day before Amber's party. When I tried to explain I just wasn't feeling it, she started shouting about how it was all Amber's fault. I couldn't care less what Amber thought about it. I don't even know how she found out. But Alayna wouldn't believe me that Amber wasn't behind my decision."

"Why didn't you tell the cops?"

"I didn't think she'd kill Amber. And I didn't want to embarrass her."

I tilted my head and searched his face. There had to be more to it than that.

He swallowed. "And I didn't want you to find out. I broke up with her because I wanted to ask you out. I was afraid you'd say no if you knew I'd been dating her." He stared down at his feet.

"We'd better get the police in here," I said through the jumble of questions and accusations bouncing around my mind.

He nodded in mute agreement and headed for the door.

~ ~ ~ ~ ~ ~ ~ ~ ~ ~

The detectives had barely been able to contain their joy at Felix's revelation. Having been handed motive on the proverbial silver platter, they raced off to the mansion to search for evidence tying Alayna to Amber's murder and Felix's poisoning. And because Felix told them Alayna usually worked until nine on Friday evenings, they were hoping to catch her still at the house. The downside of their enthusiasm was that they decided to have the available patrol units meet them at the Patrick residence, leaving no one behind to drive me back to my car.

I waited a few minutes after the Crown Victoria peeled out of the driveway to make sure they were sufficiently far away from the apartment. Then I turned toward Felix and broke the thick, awkward silence. "Well, I think I'm just going to walk back to my car. It's a nice night."

My nonchalance apparently didn't fool him. "Not a chance," he shot back instantaneously.

"What?"

He stepped toward the hallway, conveniently placing his body between me and the door. "Your pal, Detective Dumdum—"

"It's Drummond," I snapped.

"Easy, tiger," he laughed and patted his hands downward in the air. "Detective *Drummond* pulled me aside when his boss was shrieking orders into the phone. He said you were going to try to leave, and he told me, no matter what you said, I couldn't let you leave. Not until we hear that Alayna's in custody or a uniformed officer shows up at the door."

Stupid Detective Dumdum. I smoothed my expression into a smile. "Oh, come on. Since when do you listen to authority? What's he going to do about it?"

"I don't know, arrest me? He seemed pretty serious about it." Felix said without a trace of humor.

"You're not kidding, are you?"

"Come on, Rosemary, is the thought of spending time with me really so repellant?" He raised his arm and pretended to sniff at his armpit.

I tried not to smile, but a grin tugged at the corners of my mouth. Then I reminded myself about his *thing* with Alayna, and my smile evaporated. "So, what exactly was the deal with you and Alayna? Did you ..."

"Did I sleep with her? Is that what you're trying to ask?"

"Yeah," I said. I hated to admit that I cared but not knowing was driving me bananas. And unless I planned to tackle him and then make a break for the door, it looked like I was stuck here for a while. Might as well satisfy my curiosity.

He shook his head and gave me a thoughtful look. "I don't think it'd be fair to her to talk to you about that."

Huh. On the one hand, that seemed like an undue level of deference to give to a person who'd tried to kill him. On the other hand, I was encouraged to know it meant he'd be unlikely to regale any future girlfriends with the tale of the night he nearly yakked all over me. On balance, I decided I was okay with that. "That's fair," I said with a shrug.

"Thanks." He took a step closer to me. "You know, I'm not a complete douchebag."

"I don't think you're a douchebag at all. I think you're"—I paused to consider whether I wanted to be completely honest with him and decided I did—"a spoiled trust fund baby who doesn't view anyone who works for a living as his equal."

His head snapped back like I'd slapped him. I quickly added, "I don't think it's entirely your fault. You grew up filthy rich. It's what you know."

"Jeez, Rosemary, I think I'd like it better if you did think I was a douchebag," he mumbled.

The hurt in his eyes seemed genuine. I felt a measure of sympathy for him, but he needed to know. "No hard feelings, okay? I'd like to stay friends."

He wrinkled his forehead at that but, after a moment, opened his arms. I hesitated for a second—in part because I thought he might be able to feel the Kevlar vest and didn't want to get into a discussion about it. But, in the end, I hugged him.

He held me tight against his chest. I could feel his heart beating under his shirt. "Friends, huh? If you ever decide you're interested in being friends with benefits, promise you'll let me know."

I rested my head against his chest and laughed. It was true, I couldn't fault him for being an out-of-touch one percenter. And he was a reasonably decent guy—just not boyfriend material. Having him as a friend would make Los Angeles that much more palatable. "You'll be the first to know," I said in a mock serious voice.

The comfortable companionship lasted approximately ten seconds before it was interrupted by the sound of someone turning a key in the kitchen door.

I pulled back and looked up into his worried face. "Your dad?" I whispered.

"No clue."

We ended the embrace and turned to face the back of the house as the door opened and Alayna burst into the house, slamming the door shut behind her. She smiled knowingly at us. "Oh, this is perfect. You're both here." Her voice was measured but her face betrayed her emotion—she was nearly purple with rage.

Uh-oh, I thought in what had to be the internal monologue understatement of the year.

Beside me, Felix found my hand with his and gave it a reassuring squeeze. "What are you doing here?" he asked her cautiously.

She laughed frantically at that. "I think you know," she said as she walked into the sitting room and stopped about eight feet away from where we stood.

Twenty-one

THE THREE OF US STAYED motionless in an uneasy, wordless standoff for what felt like several minutes. I guess none of us had any firsthand experience in hostage situations or whatever Alayna had in mind, so we weren't sure what to do. Finally, Felix broke the silence.

"Let's go into the parlor and sit down and talk," he suggested as if there were nothing out of the ordinary about her appearance at the apartment.

Alayna narrowed her eyes and frowned. But after a moment, she nodded. "Fine. You first," she gestured toward the doorway. That's when I noticed the gleaming chef's knife in her hand. I recognized it from the kitchen. It wasn't really the best work tool, in my opinion, but it was a high-end piece of cutlery, and I happened to know that it was wickedly sharp because I'd honed it myself the night I'd made the ceviche.

My worry blossomed into something more akin to sheer panic but I forced myself to follow Felix's lead, putting one foot in front of the other, and trudged toward the seating area in the parlor. My throat was tight, my mouth was dry, and my pulse was like a trapped moth beating its wings. I lowered myself to the love seat next to Felix. I sneaked a glance at his face —pale, drawn, and serious.

In contrast, Alayna appeared to be enjoying herself. Her dark eyes shined almost merrily and she flashed us a wide smile. "So, lovebirds, do you have any idea why the police are swarming all over the mansion?" She punctuated her question by waving the knife with a flourish.

I cleared my throat to answer but Felix spoke first. "I imagine you know. But, here's a question for you— how did you manage to leave?"

She tossed her head with laughter, sending her shining hair cascading over her shoulders. "Ah, stroke of luck. Your father's lover called and asked me to run to the liquor store because the drunk was out of gin. I was delivering his booze to Antonio's house when a stream of police cars went racing past, up the hill to your house. So I continued down the hill."

"And you came here because ...?" he prompted.

Her smile widened and she pointed at me with the knife. "Because I'm guessing Rosemary here told the cops some ridiculous story about me poisoning you after she snooped around in my files today. So going home is out of the question. I'm sure there's a squad car sitting in front of my building. I considered going to the campus—lots of buildings, there—and hiding out in one of the libraries or labs. But I decided I didn't want to risk going anywhere public. Then I remembered I had a key to this place. Finding your car in the driveway was a delicious surprise. The fact that *she's* here, too, is just a bonus." She laughed—a little crazily, I thought.

I squirmed, and Felix placed a hand on my thigh, right above my knee. I'm guessing the gesture was meant to soothe me. Unfortunately, it sparked new anger in Alayna. Her face darkened and she sneered at Felix. "Save your groping for another time." His hand slid off my leg and rested on the cushion between us.

"Um, Alayna, you should know that we're not dating. Anymore, I mean." I kept my expression and voice neutral as I said the words, hoping they'd calm her down instead of further winding her up.

Her eyes sparked, and she glared at Felix. "Is that true?"

He nodded mutely.

She turned back to me. "I'd say I'm sorry, but what did you expect from him? He's a user. When he's done with you, he tosses you away like a dirty napkin."

Beside me, Felix bristled. I didn't dare look at him but I mentally willed him not to argue with her. "Is that what he did to you?" I asked softly.

For an instant, a shadow of pain replaced the rage in her face, and she blinked. "Yes, of course. He's a coward. Afraid that the vapid twit would tell his daddy about him and the Mexican girl. He didn't want to risk losing his allowance. Eh, Felix?"

I didn't give him a chance to respond and defend himself. "Is that why you killed her? Amber, I mean."

Alayna slashed the knife through the air. I pressed myself back against the couch and tensed, waiting for her to advance. But she didn't. "Do you think I've never watched TV? I'm not about to pour out my heart in a big confession to murder, Rosemary. Get a grip."

"Worth a try," I said with a casual shrug.

She shook her head in disgust.

"Well, if you aren't going to talk to us, what's the plan?" Felix asked with a surge of firmness in his voice. "If you're just going to try to carve us up and get yourself into deeper trouble, let's get on with it then." He jutted his body forward on the couch as if he might launch himself at her.

I side-eyed him. "Speak for yourself. I'd just as soon sit here and have her stare at me as get sliced into ribbons, big man." I turned back to Alayna with the friendliest expression I could muster.

"You're not so stupid, huh?" she said with a satisfied jerk of her chin in my direction.

"I hope not." I kept my eyes fixed on hers and slowly inched my foot across the floor until it was touching Felix's. Then I pressed against it with all my strength, hoping he'd pick up my signal. *Don't move. Follow my lead. I have an idea.* I thought the words as hard as I could, wishing I'd paid even the smallest bit of attention when my mom had gone through her extrasensory perception phase.

"But then you're not so smart, either. You fell for his lies, too."

I nodded my agreement. "Yeah, I did." I gave Felix's foot one final nudge and took a deep breath.

Here goes nothing.

I unfolded myself and stood up slowly with my hands outstretched. "I have to know, though, why you tried to frame me. Twice. What did I do to you?" I took a careful step forward on my unsteady legs.

"Hey!" She poked the knife toward me as if it were a cattle prod. Behind me, I heard Felix's sharp intake of breath.

I took another small step. "Take it easy, Alayna. Come on, tell me. Why me?"

She huffed in exasperation. "It's nothing personal, Rosemary. At least it *wasn't*. When you told me about Amber's menu change I was still reeling from the way she'd talked to me. She was such a bitch. As if it was an embarrassment to her that Felix would sleep with the help, especially a dirty beaner like me." Her voice shook with barely controlled rage at the memory.

"I'm so sorry," I said.

She waved away my words. "I knew that stupid gravy was supposed to have cashews and I just kept thinking, what if you screwed up and forgot to omit them? I couldn't get the idea out of my head." She clamped her jaw closed and glanced at Felix as if she'd already said too much.

I took another step before drawing her attention back to me. "But you knew I'd notice if you added them to my gravy, right? So, you didn't."

"That's right," she said with relief.

I left unsaid the part where she did leave a container of nuts in the trash to point to me and then decided to add some peanut oil to the wine. There was no point in antagonizing her about it. She wasn't going to admit to a crime.

Felix shifted on the couch and cleared his throat. "What about the Botox?"

Shut up, I screamed silently to myself.

"What about it?" she said angrily.

While she was focused on him, I closed the gap between us. I was almost close enough to reach the handle of the knife, assuming she didn't move. As I formed the thought, she waved the knife toward me. "Go sit back down," she hissed, swishing the knife sideways.

The light glinted off the blade. I almost lost my nerve and sunk to my knees. I managed not to. I planted my feet more firmly on the floor and said, "What did you do? Empty Amber's unused syringes into his water bottle?" I couldn't figure out how else she'd managed to get him to ingest the toxin.

She looked at me as if I were pathetically stupid. "Of course not. Do you think it doesn't have a taste or an odor?" Her voice dripped with condescension.

"I have no idea, honestly."

"Well it does. But his mouthwash has a very strong peppermint scent and taste."

"So you added it to his mouthwash. Smart."

She didn't respond to that comment directly. "When he asked me to pick up groceries for him and a date and bring them here, I knew you'd be the one cooking. And I knew your reputation was already in question because of Amber. So I bought scallops. Poorly prepared seafood is a common cause of food poisoning," she said with so much satisfaction that I had to stop myself from punching her in the throat.

Instead I threw a meaningful glance toward Felix. "How could you ask her to go shopping for a date for you? Don't you have any sensitivity?" I didn't have to fake the disgust in my voice because, truth be told, it was really poor form considering their past.

He started and gave me a wounded look. Just then, Alayna rounded on him with a fierce expression. "Or do you think I don't have feelings?" she shouted as she lurched forward.

This is your chance.

I released a quick prayer into the universe that the vest I was wearing was both bladeproof as well as bulletproof and snaked out my hand to grab her right wrist. I yanked hard, pulling her off-balance. She stumbled toward me with the knife flailing between us and a look of pure shock painted across her face.

"Are you crazy?" she yelled.

Apparently, I thought.

Then three things happened. In the chaos, I don't know if they all happened at once or just one right after the other. Felix let out a wordless war noise, threw himself off the couch and toward us, and tackled Alayna. Alayna slashed the knife through my abdomen. And the front door splintered, crashing inward with a tremendous noise. Loud voices and pounding feet followed.

Someone flipped on the overhead lights. I squinted into the glare, overwhelmed by the brightness, the shouting, the swirling motion all around me. Then the base of my skull bounced off the hardwood floor and everything went dark and silent.

~ ~ ~ ~ ~ ~ ~ ~ ~ ~

I came to on the loveseat. A paramedic with curly red hair was taking my pulse. I surveyed the room. Two uniformed police officers were hanging yellow crime scene tape over the entrance to the house. Felix, apparently unscathed, was sitting in one of the Queen Anne chairs, giving a statement to Detective Sullivan. I nearly went into shock when I saw Pat standing behind him, a fatherly hand on Felix's shoulder.

My pulse must have reacted, too, because the paramedic met my eyes. "Hey, you're awake," she said. "Take it easy, now."

I pushed myself up on my elbows and craned my neck. There was no sign of Alayna. Or the knife. I inhaled and my stomach muscles burned in protest. I gasped, and the medic pushed me gently back to a supine position. "No more of that," she said. "You took a pretty good knock on the head. And you have a superficial abdominal wound." She lifted my blouse to show me a large white dressing covering most of my stomach. A large blotch of blood colored the center of the dressing.

I was about to tell her there was nothing superficial about it from my end, when Sergeant Bentley walked in from the kitchen holding the protective vest I'd been wearing. She beelined toward me.

"Thanks a lot, Ms. Field. Now I have to requisition a new female vest. Look at this thing." She waved it at me, the slashed fabric dangling in ribbons. I wondered how much a bulletproof vest cost.

I was about to apologize but she burst into laughter. "Don't look so serious. I'm just busting your chops."

"Oh." I managed a weak smile. I scanned the room again.

"You looking for Ramirez?" she asked.

"Yes," I said, although it wasn't the whole truth. I realized I was also looking for Detective Drummond.

"She's on her way downtown with Detective Drummond," she told me.

My relief that Alayna was in custody mingled with an emotion that felt an awful lot like disappointment that Detective Drummond wasn't around. "Good," I said, setting aside my feelings about Detective Drummond for later analysis – preferably with my sisters, over drinks.

"It is good. And you're damned lucky. Erin here says you're going to be fine. The vest protected your vital organs, which, just so you know, wasn't a given. It's bulletproof, not bladeproof. Just a pro tip for next time."

"There won't be a next time," I promised as I touched my tender stomach.

"Good. Now, the bigger concern is that you lost consciousness. We're probably going to have to take you to the hospital for observation to make sure you weren't concussed. Right, Erin?"

The other woman nodded. "That's right. Let's do this cognitive assessment and then we'll get you on your way to the hospital."

I opened my mouth to protest that I was fine and just wanted to go home, but Sergeant Bentley cut me off before I could get the first word out. "No. Uh-uh. Not up for discussion. You're going to the hospital." Her voice conveyed finality. I'm sure overreacting to minor injuries was also part of their CYA efforts regarding civilians who got mixed up in police actions. And I was too tired to argue.

From across the room, Felix caught my eye and smiled before turning back to Detective Sullivan and her no doubt relentless questions. Sergeant Bentley patted my arm and drifted away to talk to a pair of forensic investigators who appeared in the doorway, clutching their kits in their hands.

I was dutifully answering Erin's questions about current events when Pat walked over and stood about a foot away, clearing his throat. After a moment, Erin flashed me a bright smile. "I think you're gonna live. I'll be back in a minute to move you to the stretcher, but it looks like this gentleman wants a word."

She gathered her equipment, closed her bag, and walked over to join the cluster of people in the doorway.

I raised my eyes to Pat and waited.

"What you did was very brave. And stupid."

I couldn't agree more, but his pronouncement didn't seem to call for a response.

He shuffled his feet. "I understand from Felix that you probably saved his life. So ... thank you," he said stiffly.

"No thanks needed. I was trying to save myself, too." I smiled to let him off the hook. Watching him awkwardly attempt gratitude as if it required superhuman effort was making *me* start to sweat.

"Yes, well." He paused. "Okay then."

He turned to walk away but I called after him. "Wait, Pat. Do you know why the police came back here? How'd they know Alayna was here?"

He smiled proudly over his shoulder. "Antonio figured it out. Alayna was delivering a package to him when several police cars went screaming by, headed toward the house. He said she reacted very strangely. She raced back to her car and took off down the through the canyon. He flagged down one of the stragglers in the police convoy and got a lift to the house to tell them what happened. That junior detective—the guy who's partnered with Detective Sullivan—pieced it together, and Antonio gave him a lift back here in one of his faster cars. And, well, I suppose you know the rest."

"Sort of. Tell Antonio I said thank you," I said with emotion. I didn't want to think what might have happened if the cavalry hadn't shown up.

"I'll do that." Pat turned back to face me fully. "Your job's waiting for you if you want it back," he said.

I thought about that for a moment. Then I gave my head a small shake, which I immediately regretted because the movement sent a searing pain through my skull. "Thanks, Pat. But no thanks. I'm starting my own business."

He raised one silver eyebrow in response to that and then shrugged. "Well, then, good for you. Best of luck to you, Rosemary."

Twenty-two

I WAS STARING AT THE ceiling of my hospital room, too keyed up to sleep but too drained to read a book or watch reruns on basic cable when someone eased the door open very slowly, the way you do when you're trying not to make any noise.

I turned to face the hallway. "I'm awake," I called.

The door swung open, and Detective Drummond peered in at me, backlit by the dim light from the hall. "Are you up for a visit? I'll keep it short."

"Come on in," I said. I hit the button to raise the bed so I was sort of sitting up and arranged the thin, scratchy sheet over my chest.

He dragged the metal chair from the corner of the room over to my bedside and pulled it close. As he sat down, he eyed me closely. "How are you feeling?"

"Bored," I told him. "I'm fine. I just have to cool my heels here until morning to prove I don't have a concussion."

Relief washed over his face in a wave, and he exhaled a long, ragged breath. He reached for my hand. "Thank God. I've been so worried about you." His shoulders sagged as if he'd just put down a heavy weight.

"Didn't anyone tell you?"

"I've been busy processing Ms. Ramirez. I haven't had a chance to check on you. Last I saw you, you were unconscious on the floor, bleeding." His voice cracked.

I squeezed his hand and smiled up at him. "I'm totally fine," I promised.

He reached out and stroked my hair. "The log had a notation that you'd been transported to Ronald Reagan Medical Center with no other notes. I was imagining all sorts of things."

We smiled at each other in the glow of the medical monitoring equipment. Ghastly green isn't really my color, but at the moment, I didn't care that I probably looked like a washed out hag. It was so good to see him. My grin threatened to split my face, and my heart felt all bursty with emotion.

Then his smile faded. "That was really stupid, you know. Rushing a woman who had a knife. Boneheaded, even."

I bristled. "Hey—"

He put a finger against my lips to stop my tirade before it even started. "Listen. You can't go around scaring me like that. From now on, you're going to have to be less brave and more careful."

From now on?

I searched his face but couldn't read him. Finally I said, "Don't worry, I don't plan on wrestling with any murderers in the future."

"Good answer." He raised himself off the chair and cupped my face with his hands. My heart galloped at his touch, and I prayed it wouldn't set off an alarm on one of the monitors behind me. "Rosemary, I—" he began in a raw voice, trailing a finger along my cheekbone.

Then the overhead lights blazed on. I winced and squeezed my eyes shut. He dropped his hands and jumped back like my face was on fire.

When I blinked my eyes open, he was planted firmly in the chair, and Detective Sullivan was standing in the middle of the room, clutching a clipboard.

"Uh, hi?" I said weakly, wishing she'd just go away, so he could get back to tenderly caressing my face.

"Ms. Field," she said with a curt nod. "How are you feeling?"

"I'm fine."

"Glad to hear it." Her gaze shifted to the seat next to my bed. "Detective Drummond, I didn't realize you'd be here. I thought you signed out."

He cleared his throat. "I just wanted to check on Ms. Field," he said as he stood.

Don't go, I thought.

"I wish you'd told me. I could have saved myself the trip," she answered with a tired sigh. I turned back to look at her and noticed the dark circles forming under her eyes. She was human, after all.

"Sorry, boss," he mumbled, inching toward the door.

I let out a little sigh of my own.

"I wanted to let you know that I've spoken to your sisters," Detective Sullivan said, bringing her attention back to me. "They're both making arrangements to come out from the East Coast."

"That's not necessary," I protested.

"Probably not," she agreed. Then she cracked the tiniest of smiles. "However, they were both—how should I say this?—agitatedly insistent that you needed them."

I had to admit that agitatedly insistent sounded like Sage and Thyme. Arguing would be futile. "Okay," I said. "Thanks for letting me know."

"You're welcome. I also wanted to let you know that Ms. Ramirez has an outstanding warrant from Juarez, Mexico, and isn't going to be able to get bail. She'll be held until trial."

I raised an eyebrow at the news of the criminal past, but I was more interested in the part where Alayna wouldn't be out roaming the streets. "Good," I said.

"Good night, Ms. Field," Detective Drummond said from the doorway in an impersonal voice.

For a moment I wondered if I'd hallucinated the tenderness that had just past between us. I *was* getting intravenous pain medication, after all. But as I looked up quizzically, he quirked his mouth into a quick smile and threw me a wink. Then he disappeared through the door.

I stifled a sigh and turned my attention back to Detective Sullivan, who seemed committed to running through the items on her clipboard before she left.

Twenty-three

Two weeks later

I GROANED AND SMASHED MY pillow over my head. For a moment I thought I was having a bad dream. Or déjà vu. I'd been up way too late the night before, catering a reunion dinner until eleven and seeing my sisters off with one last night of cocktails and dancing before they flew back East. Now it was seven o'clock on a Saturday and somebody was pounding on my front door. The last time this had happened, I'd spent my day at the police station. I groaned and eased myself out from under the blanket, careful not to disturb the lump curled up at my feet.

I hurried to the door, pulling my wild hair into a loose knot at the back of my head in a movement that made my arms ache. *Everything* ached these days. The long hours of catering six days a week left me stiff, sore, and ridiculously happy. I was already looking forward to tonight's event—a benefit dinner for Rescue Haven.

I tugged my thin tank top down over my shorts and pulled open the door.

Detective Drummond stood in the hallway with a small grocery bag in one hand. He was wearing street clothes and a wide smile. "Good morning," he said cheerily, as if his appearance at my front door were an everyday occurrence.

"Um ... hi?" I mumbled uncertainly.

"Can I come in?" he asked already halfway through the doorway.

"I guess so. Do you promise not to arrest me?" I cracked as I shut the door and turned to face him.

His smiled vanished and he spoke in his cop voice. "Well I don't know that I can do that, Rosemary. I understand you're harboring a fugitive."

My sleepy brain was still trying to process that statement when Mona Lisa came bounding out of the bedroom and nearly knocked him into the wall with a flurry of dog kisses.

"She must have recognized your voice," I said while he crouched on the floor and gave her a vigorous belly rub.

He smiled up at me. "I thought your lease prohibits pets?"

"It does. But it turns out the super is a widower who misses both his wife's cooking and his recently departed canine companion. I make Mr. Rizzo a pan of lasagna every Sunday. In exchange, he looks the other way. Shoot, he does more than that. He takes Mona Lisa out for a walk when an event runs late."

Detective Drummond scratched the pup's floppy ears and then rose to stand next to me.

"I was surprised when I showed up for my shift at the rescue center last week and she was gone," he said as he handed me the grocery bag, I peeked inside—bagels, cream cheese, and a peanut butter dog cookie.

"You want some coffee?" I asked.

"That'd be great. I figured I better bring breakfast unless the state of your refrigerator has changed dramatically since the last time I was here."

"It hasn't," I assured him as I moved into the kitchen and got busy with the coffeemaker. He followed me in, trailed by the dog, and fed her the treat.

"I'm glad you adopted her," he said.

"Me, too." I smiled down at her where she lay making short work of the dog biscuit. I raised my eyes to find Detective Drummond standing closer to me than societal norms would dictate. My heart rate ticked up a notch. "I'm catering a dinner for Rescue Haven tonight. You should, uh, come." I smiled nervously and rested my elbows against the counter.

"That's why I'm here," he said. "I don't have a date."

I chewed on my lower lip and tried to figure out what he was getting at. "I'm guessing Detective Sullivan doesn't have plans. You should ask her," I ventured, trying to keep a straight face.

"One, Lisa isn't as terrible as you make her out to be. Two, she's married. Three, she isn't the girl I'd like to ask."

"Oh? Then ask the girl you're interested in, Detective—"

"Didn't I ask you to call me Dave?" he said. He stared hard at me, and I stared back, mesmerized by the way the gold in his eyes picked up the sunlight.

"Right. Sorry, Dave." I rummaged in the candy bowl on the edge of the counter and popped a mint into my mouth, suddenly very conscious of the fact that I hadn't yet brushed my teeth. I extended the bowl toward him. "Mint?"

He took one, keeping his eyes locked on mine. "And the girl I wanted to ask, turns out she's gotta work tonight."

I inhaled sharply and nearly sucked the peppermint into my windpipe in the process. "Oh, yeah?"

"Yeah." He braced his hands on the counter, one on each side of me and leaned forward with a grin.

My heart jumped again. I swallowed hard and reached out a hand and felt one of his rock-hard biceps. Then I nodded. "You'll do."

He arched an eyebrow. "For what?"

"Since you can't get a date, you can come with me. I could use some muscle to set up and tear down the tables. You could probably be trusted to pass trays of appetizers, too," I said in a matter-of-fact voice as I trailed my hand along his arm.

His smile spread lazily and he dipped his head. A deep dimple revealed itself in his chin.

I reached up and laced my fingers together behind his head. "So, what do you say? You interested?"

In answer, he covered my mouth with a kiss. I leaned forward, my lips meeting his hungrily. He pressed himself against me, pushing me back against the counter with the weight of his hips.

"Oh, I'm interested," he breathed.

I arched my neck back to appraise him. "Good." I ran my hands along his muscular arms again. "I'll just have to make sure you're up for the job."

He trailed his mouth along my ear. "How do you intend to do that?" he asking, nipping my ear lightly with his teeth.

I was losing my ability to think, let alone speak. "Uh, I'll have to confirm your stamina," I managed.

He reached out with one hand and pushed the spaghetti straps of my tank top off my left shoulder and then my right. "Stamina, huh?" he echoed, moving his mouth along my neck to my bare shoulder.

"Uh-huh. Also, flexibility," I said, fumbling with the buttons on his shirt.

"Stamina and flexibility. Anything else?"

"Creativity is very important." My thighs began to tremble, which he had to have noticed because his right leg was pressed between them.

"I think I've got it. I'm ready for my interview," he said.

I undid the remaining buttons on his shirt, and it fell open. His chest rippled with muscles. I swallowed hard and ran my hands along his bare skin.

He caught my hand. "One more thing, before this goes any further."

"What's that?" I asked, suddenly uncertain.

"Promise me you aren't going to make that damned gravy again." Then he laughed, a throaty, full-bodied laugh, and pulled me tight. My hips bumped up against his.

"Detective Drummond, you've got yourself a deal."

He narrowed his eyes. "I thought I told you to call me Dave."

I let a slow smile play across my lips before answering. "Why don't you try and make me."

AUTHOR'S NOTE

Thanks so much for picking up Rosemary's adventure! Next up in the We Sisters Three Series, it's middle sister Sage's turn in *Sage of Innocence* (slated for later in 2015), followed by Thyme's story in *Thyme to Live* (no date yet set).

I'd love to hear from you by email at melissa@melissafmiller.com. Or you can stop by my Facebook page for book updates, cover reveals, pithy quotes about coffee, and general time-wasting at https://www.facebook.com/authormelissafmiller. To be the first to know when I have a new release, sign up for my email newsletter at www.melissafmiller.com. I only send emails when I have book news—I promise.

ABOUT THE AUTHOR

Melissa F. Miller is a *USA TODAY* bestselling author and a commercial litigator. She has practiced in the offices of international law firms in Pittsburgh, PA and Washington, D.C. She and her husband now practice law together in their two-person firm in South Central Pennsylvania, where they live with their three children, a lazy hound dog, and three overactive gerbils. When not in court or on the playground, Melissa writes crime fiction. Like some of her characters, she drinks entirely too much coffee; unlike any of her characters, she cannot kill you with her bare hands.

ALSO BY MELISSA F. MILLER

The Sasha McCandless Series

•*Irreparable Harm*
•*Inadvertent Disclosure*
•*Irretrievably Broken*
•*Indispensable Party*
•*Lovers and Madmen:*
A Sasha McCandless Novella
•*Improper Influence*
•*A Marriage of True Minds:*
A Sasha McCandless Novella
•*Irrevocable Trust*
•*Irrefutable Evidence*

The Aroostine Higgins Series

•*Critical Vulnerability*
•*Chilling Effect*

Made in the USA
Lexington, KY
19 April 2016